HAPPY HOURS

HAPPY

HOURS

Gary Smith

Harmony Books   New York

Published by Harmony Books, a division of Crown Publishers, Inc., 225 Park Avenue South, New York, New York 10003 and represented in Canada by the Canadian MANDA Group.
HARMONY and colophon are trademarks of Crown Publishers, Inc.
Manufactured in the United States of America

Library of Congress Cataloging-in-Publication Data
Smith, Gary (Gary Michael)
  Happy hours.
  I. Title.
PS3569.M53518H3   1987   813'.54   86-25755

ISBN 0-517-56523-4
10 9 8 7 6 5 4 3 2 1

First Edition

To the memory of my parents,
Harold Louis Smith and Kathryn Duncan Smith;
and to the memory of Susan Kirby Agnew

I would like to thank Jeff Murray for his advice,
and Teresa for her long support

1 · *His Lips*

Every night Willy waited by the big picture window for his father's car to come out of the darkness and into the driveway.

Willy's mother would have already set a pitcher of cocktails on the coffee table in the living room. Seconds before his father walked through the front door Willy would hurry into hiding, and night after night he ran to the same spot. Halfway up the staircase he'd fall to his knees and tuck his body and make himself invisible. That his head poked through the banister posts didn't matter. Willy was invisible, and when his father walked by the staircase with a chill still on his overcoat he wouldn't see anything out of the ordinary. He never did. Not seeing was part of the game.

At six P.M. or thereabouts his parents had cocktails. Two apiece, like aspirin, bringing momentary relief from whatever the day had delivered. This was their time alone before dinner with the kids. Willy's older brother Matt, who could be found in the den watching television in a near trance, would eventually greet their father at the dinner table. But four-year-old Willy, hiding on a step halfway up the staircase, could never wait until dinner to see his father. Dinner was too far away.

With the greatest of effort he'd stay on the staircase and spy on his parents. The waiting was hard and thrilling and made little Willy, curled and wound tight as he was, nearly piss his pants. He'd allow his parents a few minutes in privacy—that was part of the game, too—but once his father reached for the glass pitcher to pour a second drink, Willy would spring to his feet. Like some high-strung domestic animal he'd bound down the stairs and across the living-room floor and leap forty-pounds-heavy into his father's lap. Willy needed to be near his father, to get as close as he could manage. The longer he waited on the staircase, the longer he let his parents sip their cocktails, the closer he'd be able to get to his father.

Willy would press himself into his father's chest and the softness of his belly and listen to the sound of his father's deep voice—not the words his father spoke, just the sound he made. And he'd feel the heat from his father's body and feel the steady rhythm of his breathing. But most of all, most of all, Willy liked to move in close and smell the cocktail on his father's lips. The cocktail made his father happy. When Willy's father was happy, Willy was happy.

2 · *Human Kindness*

When Vee was five years old her baby brother Patrick died just like that. In the space of fourteen hours, the time it then took to fly from New York to Los Angeles, Patrick had gone from his playpen to a hospital room, and from a hospital room to the emergency room, and from the emergency room to the morgue. Two days later he was underground.

While Vee may have been too young to grieve, she was old enough to wonder. She'd been told Patrick had died, but where did he *go?* Was he allowed to take any of his things with him when he left? Did he cry?

Vee's parents were at a loss for answers, but more than anything else they were overwhelmed by death, by an obscure viral infection that could not be explained or even named. To name was to know, to have something to blame. Vee's father tried to answer her questions, but he could barely concentrate, he had trouble thinking, even remembering his phone number. "I don't know, honey," was all he was able to say to Vee. Every question received the same reply. "I don't *know*, honey."

The family doctor cautioned Vee's parents that the death of a child had been known to pull apart the happiest of couples. The most important thing, he said, was to be good to each other. Later on you'll feel better. You're both young, you can have other children. . . .

But Vee's parents didn't want another child, not if another child might mean another loss, however slim the chance. They still had Vee. She was bright and independent, she'd be fine. They'd all be fine. But they took the doctor's advice about being good to each other, and six days after Patrick's death, four days after the burial, they were on a DC-7 bound for Lisbon. They stayed three weeks.

Vee was in her first year of grade school and left in the charge of Elizabeth Akorn, a spinster who had lived in the community all her life. Vee's parents had interviewed several people for the job, and Miss Akorn, a retired schoolteacher, seemed the best of the lot, though of course it was difficult to tell, they hardly had time to acquaint themselves with the woman.

On the evening of their departure for Portugal, while waiting for Miss Akorn to arrive, Vee's parents talked between themselves in the foyer. Suitcases with name tags attached to handles stood by the front door. Vee had been sent to her room upstairs to draw a picture for Miss Akorn, but she was still able to listen to her parents talking downstairs. She overheard her father joke, "I hope this Akorn lady doesn't turn out to be a nut." Vee's mother apparently found the remark funny, for she laughed and laughed, the first real laughter in the house since Patrick had died.

But where was the punch line? Vee understood a nut to be a crazy person. Why would her parents leave her alone with a nut? Only minutes after her mother and father left for Idlewild airport, Vee confronted Miss Akorn.

"Daddy said he hoped you weren't a nut. You aren't, are you?"

"What was that?" Miss Akorn said sharply. "What did I hear you say?"

"A *nut*," Vee said. "Daddy said he hoped you weren't a nut."

Elizabeth Akorn had been teased about her surname ever since she was Vee's age. *If Libby Akorn got run over by a truck, what type of food would she be? Acorn squash!*

"I want you bathed and in bed in five minutes," Miss Akorn told Vee.

"But I get to stay up and watch TV," Vee said.

"Not tonight you don't, missy. Tonight you go to bed."

Vee washed one of her hands and one side of her face and tried to brush her teeth on only one side of her mouth. Maybe Miss Akorn was crazy and maybe she wasn't, but until Vee made up her mind she was only going to do half of what was asked of her.

Vee soon discovered, though, that Miss Akorn wasn't much different from anyone else she knew, just older. She set out Vee's clothes in the morning, walked her to the bus stop, waited for her to come back home in the afternoon. She fussed over Vee's drawings and played spelling games with her during meals. If not exactly friends, Vee and Miss Akorn had at least stopped irritating each other.

Every night before bed Vee was allowed to draw in her sketch pad and watch TV in the downstairs den, which was actually a finished basement her parents had paneled with cedar and decorated with a nautical theme. After putting the dinner dishes in the kitchen sink, Miss Akorn would join Vee, the two of them seated side by side in canvas captain's chairs in front of the large black and white Philco set with the brass ship's compass on top of the cabinet. Every thirty minutes or so Miss Akorn would mix herself a drink behind the bar at the back of the den. Simply holding a loaded highball glass in her hand could restore the vigor the day had drained from her. Sweet dark rum was her drink of preference, though there were so many different bottles to choose from behind the bar that she found herself cautiously experimenting. Maybe Vee's father wouldn't begrudge her a simple drink at the end of a day. He might even commend her good sense, but then again he might think otherwise. He might even be offended, Miss Akorn couldn't tell with men. To cover herself she watered the alcohol to give the bottles the appearance of not having been tampered with. She was sure never to add too much water to a bottle, nor to water any one bottle more than a single time.

Vee noticed Miss Akorn bent over the sink behind the bar, and, curious as always, asked what she was doing. Flushed from her third highball, Miss Akorn responded warmly. "Why I'm freshening up the bottle, child." Carefully, she added the merest trickle of tap water to a fifth of Glenlivet. "These liquors are very delicate and need to be freshened from time to time."

"Like flowers?" Vee said.

"That's right, just like cut flowers in a vase. I'm not really supposed to be doing this, you know. I was only told to look after you, but then I thought I'd go ahead and do a little extra for your father."

"As a surprise?"

"More like a courtesy, honey. A kindness. Now don't go spilling a word about this to your daddy. It's just something I'm doing. A kindness isn't a kindness if you expect to be rewarded. Do we understand each other?"

The evening Vee's parents were scheduled to return home, Miss Akorn was upstairs vacuuming the living-room carpet and dusting the venetian blinds, chores she'd put off until the very last minute. She'd spent her life in a brick schoolhouse, after all, not a suburban home. Housekeeping was hardly one of her specialties.

Vee had been sent to the den to watch TV, but upon hearing the vacuum upstairs decided she'd do her own to help out. Miss Akorn hadn't really been such bad company. She'd do something for Miss Akorn and she'd do something for her father, both at the same time. She'd already drawn a picture for her mother and taped it to the refrigerator door. She'd drawn a picture for Patrick too, burying it in the flower bed in the backyard beneath mulch and loose soil. At the cemetery she'd seen flowers everywhere. Maybe if she put the drawing in the ground, Patrick would have a better chance of receiving it.

Vee got behind the bar and gathered as many bottles as she could find and lined them up in neat rows next to the sink. There were bottles of dry sherry and apricot brandy, bottles of bourbon and rye and blended scotch, bottles of imported liqueurs and cordials with colorful labels and sticky caps. Every bottle she could open was opened, and then topped off, beyond the neck and to the very lip, with a rush of water from the tap.

Vee was mindful not to tell Miss Akorn what she had done. Being kind was its own reward.

3 · *Television*

At a quarter to eleven, long after he should have been asleep, Willy slipped into dungarees and sneakers and opened his bedroom door a crack. His parents had packed him off to bed at nine, but on this soft warm night in May, a Friday night, Willy had a date to keep with Mickey.

Stealing away was easier than it was hard, but that didn't make Willy any less nervous. His parents were in their own bedroom, the door latched. He could hear their television set, the portable Motorola that sat on an aluminum stand near the foot of the bed, as he snuck past their room. Matt was in his own room down the hall, door ajar, lights out.

After creeping down the stairs, careful of steps that might make noise, Willy threaded his way through the unlit house, stopping and listening as he entered each room to see if he was being followed. He told himself nothing would jump out at him, that furniture was still furniture, even if it looked dangerous in the dark. He told himself night rhymed with light, *night light*, and left the house by the back kitchen door. Once outside he ran to his bike, which was leaning against the side of the garage.

Willy and Matt and their parents lived in a split-level house in a sprawling tract development on the North Shore of Long

Island. Each house in the tract sat on a half-acre plot. Mickey and his family lived in a ranch house in the same development, not quite a quarter of a mile away. Willy and Mickey had agreed to meet at eleven o'clock, the signal being a tapping on Mickey's bedroom window. Willy carried a quarter in his pocket for the tapping. Their plan seemed bold, and to them it was, though in fact the adventure went no further than riding their bikes through the neighborhood in the still of a late spring night. Willy was nine years old and Mickey ten. They were best friends.

Willy turned into Mickey's driveway and laid his bike in the cropped grass, which was already wet and slippery with dew. He followed a slate path along the perimeter of the house until he reached the backyard. Except for a narrow band of light from the master bedroom, the house was a box of darkness.

Willy left the path and pressed close to the back of the house. Through haste or negligence the curtains in the master bedroom had not been completely drawn, leaving a gap. As Willy passed the window on his way to Mickey's bedroom, he stopped and peered in. What he first saw was a television set near the foot of a large bed, a set not so different from the one in his parents' bedroom. He turned his head and there was Mickey's father, Mr. Dekker, reclining in bed and propped up by a pillow, bare-chested, a sheet pulled to his waist. On a table beside the bed stood a shaded lamp, and beneath the lamp Willy saw a tray holding a green liquor bottle, an ice bucket, and two glasses.

More curious than uneasy, and with his chin level with the windowsill, Willy watched Mr. Dekker watch TV. A moment passed and then a blast of light filled the bedroom. Willy ducked down before peering over the windowsill again, only to find Mrs. Dekker emerging from the master bathroom. As she closed the door behind her the bright light vanished and Willy stared in disbelief. Except for a pair of furry slippers and a red bath towel wrapped turban-fashion around her hair, Mrs. Dekker was naked. Willy had seen pictures of women in *Playboy*, but never before had he seen a naked woman in the flesh, and the difference startled him. Flat pictures held in the hand had not prepared him for the staggering life-size fullness of Mrs. Dekker. His eyes raced over her face and breasts and came to rest on the luxuriant black patch between her legs, black as any black he'd ever seen. He jerked his head away from the window and looked off into deep backyard darkness, knowing he couldn't leave. Mickey would have to wait. They'd meet some other night, some other time.

Mrs. Dekker sat on the edge of the bed near the bedside table and drank from her glass. She and Mr. Dekker were talking, though Willy couldn't hear what they said. As Mrs. Dekker leaned over to put her glass back on the tray, Mr. Dekker slid his hand under her arm and cupped one of her breasts. Both of them laughed easily, and Willy felt a delightful shiver run through the seat of his pants. Mrs. Dekker then turned to face her husband and lifted the sheet from his body. He was naked too, Willy had already guessed as much, but the real surprise was the size of his prick, which stood up and away from his body and was impossibly large.

Willy jerked his head from the window again. Mr. Dekker's prick was longer and thicker than any he'd imagined. He reached into his pants and felt his own, unexpectedly stiff but somehow pint-sized, delicate, no wider than a grown man's finger.

Mrs. Dekker used both of her hands to touch and massage her husband, and then she bent over his belly and kissed him. Willy was stunned all over again to see Mr. Dekker's prick disappearing inside his wife's mouth. He pulled away from the window for a minute or more, hardly able to think, and when he finally looked back he discovered Mrs. Dekker straddling her husband and seated in his lap. She lifted herself up and then sat back down, up and then down, fast and slow, bouncing as if a child.

Watching them, Willy quickly decided, was almost like being tickled. He didn't know how much more he could take. His eyes wandered over the bedroom, avoiding the attached bodies, and fell on the bedside table, on the ice bucket and green liquor bottle. J&B, he read, his lips moving, forming the letters without actually sounding them. J&B was scotch. He knew this because sometimes his mother and father drank J&B. Sometimes they brought drinks to the bedroom and then watched TV behind a closed door. His parents were watching TV right now.

Willy backed away from the Dekkers' bedroom window and followed the slate path to the front of the house. He picked his bike up from the wet grass, but instead of hopping on the seat and speeding home, he walked the bike along the street, not trusting his sense of balance.

4 · *Shadow of Love*

Early one January afternoon Vee's father came home from his law office in the city with a case of laryngitis. He met his wife coming out the front door as he was going in. This was a Tuesday, her day as a volunteer at the local library. She said she'd stop at the A&P after she finished at the library and then be home about six. She said, "Why don't you change into something warm, Phil. Watch the afternoon movie." He put his hand to his throat and whispered, "Maybe I'll do that. Vee can keep me company when she gets home from school."

Vee's father changed into pajamas and slippers and found a folded blanket in the hall closet upstairs and wrapped the blanket around his shoulders. Then he padded downstairs to the den and flicked on the TV. Before settling into an easy chair he went to his study adjoining the den and picked a pipe from the pipe rack on his desk. Tobacco would aggravate his throat, but at least he could keep a pipe in his hand.

Vee was delighted to find her father home so early in the day. He took the train to the city each morning before she was even out of bed, and often didn't get home until eight in the evening. Vee's mother served dinner twice each night—once for Vee at six-thirty, and once again for herself and Vee's father at eight-thirty.

"Hi, honey," Vee's father whispered. He was watching a gangster movie on TV.

"What's the matter with your voice?" Vee asked.

"Laryngitis."

"Laryngitis?" Vee imitated her father's whisper. "What's laryngitis?"

"Nothing serious. Probably from talking too much in court."

"But what is it?"

He pointed to his throat. "Inflammation of the larynx. Hey, are you trying to sound like me?"

Vee laughed and sat in the captain's chair next to her father. Mimicking his voice reminded her of shadows. When you walked in the sun your shadow followed you. Sometimes Vee imagined her shadow would get loose and wander off by itself, doing things she would like to do. By mimicking the sound of her father's strained whisper, she made her voice like the shadow of his voice.

During a commercial break in the movie Vee's father said he'd like a hot drink. "Do you think you can make one for me, honey?" he asked.

"Of course," Vee whispered in her shadow voice.

"Good girl. This is what you have to do. Listen carefully. Go upstairs to the kitchen and fill the teakettle with fresh water and put it on the stove. While you're waiting for the water to heat up, get one of my coffee mugs from the cabinet. Are you with me so far?"

Vee nodded.

"Good. Then go to the liquor cabinet under the sink and get a jigger glass—"

"Why can't I make you a drink from the bar down here?"

"Because we don't have hot water down in the den, honey. We don't have a lot of things down here that we need to make this particular drink. Now listen carefully. Get a jigger glass—"

"Is a jigger glass a shot glass?"

Vee's father rubbed his throat. "Do you want to do this or not?" he whispered.

"Yes," Vee said in her natural voice. "I get a jigger glass. Is a jigger glass a shot glass?"

Vee's father nodded. "You get a *jigger* glass and you fill the jigger glass with whiskey, with Jack Daniels, which is in the liquor cabinet, and you pour the whiskey into the coffee mug. All right? Then you go to the refrigerator and take out a lemon and slice the lemon in half. Easy, right? You help your mother chop vegetables all the time. Then you squeeze juice from the lemon into the mug, and after that you take a spoonful of honey—do you know where the honey is?"

"On the counter next to the sugar bowl."

"Good girl. You take a spoonful of honey and you drop it into the coffee mug, spoon and all. By this time the water on the stove should be hot enough to pour into the mug. Then you stir it all up with the spoon you used for the honey and you bring it down here to me and I'll give you a big kiss and we'll be friends for life. Okay? That's not so tough, is it?" He sat back in the easy chair and gathered the blanket around his shoulders. "The movie's starting again," he whispered. "Go upstairs now."

Ten minutes later Vee returned to the den and handed her father the drink. "What do you call this thing?" she said in her shadow voice.

"It's called a hot toddy, but you can call it whatever you like. What would you like to call it?"

"Hot *tooty*," Vee said.

"Hot tooty it is. Cheers."

Vee lifted an imaginary mug to her mouth. "Cheers," she said. "What does a hot tooty do?"

"Well, let's see. The hot water warms me, and the whiskey lifts my spirits, and the honey and lemon soothe my throat. Let's watch the movie now."

Half an hour later Vee's father asked for another drink. Vee repeated the formula for making the toddy, though she forgot to heat the water in the teakettle while going through the other steps. By the time the water was hot and Vee back downstairs in the den with the fresh drink in her hand, her father was asleep. He'd taken off his slippers and tucked his feet beneath the blanket and sat comfortably curled in the easy chair.

"Are you asleep, Daddy?"

He didn't stir. Vee took off her shoes and stepped into her father's slippers and sat down, but then she got up and gently pried the pipe from her father's hand. She sat down again, but then she got up and reached for the toddy on the end table next to the easy chair.

"I don't feel so good," she said in her shadow voice. "I've got laryngitis." She looked at her sleeping father. "It's nice to come home and have my girl take care of me. Thanks, Vee. You make the best hot tooties in the world." She sipped from the toddy and sucked on the empty pipe.

When the phone rang in her father's study Vee shuffled off in his slippers to answer it. She took the toddy and the pipe with her.

"Hello?" she whispered in her shadow voice.

"Phil? This is Vic. You sound terrible, worse than this morning. Look, I'm sorry to bother you, but I got another call from Hoover, the guy who wants to sue the steak house on Third Avenue. He's pressing us to take the case. I don't know, but my guess is that there isn't a hell of a lot of money here. I don't trust the guy, anyway. If you want I can stall until we've talked more about it, but I'd just as soon say no right now and lose the guy. What do you want to do?"

"Lose him," Vee whispered.

"Good, I'll call him back and tell him we're busy. You going to be in tomorrow?"

Vee said, "I don't think so. Vee's taking care of me."

"Good for her. That's what kids are for. Listen, we'll talk tomorrow."

Vee hung up the phone and took another sip from the toddy, which had begun to flush her face and make her feel warm. She was sitting at her father's desk. On the far corner of the desk top, next to the rack of pipes, was a small photograph propped in a gray cardboard frame. Vee reached for the photo and held it close to her face. In the picture, which she had seen many times but could not place, she was a little girl standing between her parents. The three of them wore swimsuits, and her mother wore a sun hat with a wide brim. Vee's father held one of her hands and Vee's mother held her other hand. In the background was a beach and high dunes—the South Shore of Long Island her father had told her. But what beach, Vee wondered, what was its name? She could never remember. In the picture, Vee's parents were smiling and gazing into the distance, presumably at the ocean, while Vee, looking directly at the camera, was squinting.

The photo always made Vee uncomfortable in a way she found hard to explain. Once she had asked her father if he would replace the picture with another, one where they all looked happy. "But you had a great time that day," her father had said. Vee couldn't remember whether she'd had a great time or not, and now all that was left of that day was a photograph of her looking as if she might cry or start screaming.

She slid open the middle drawer of her father's desk and picked out a ballpoint pen, but then put it down again in favor of a pencil. Holding her tongue between her teeth, she carefully drew a smile on the face of the girl in the photograph.

"You had a great time that day," she said in her natural voice.

5 · *A Small Loan*

Four of them huddled beneath a tall pine in the woods at the edge of the housing development. Willy's shoes were damp from a drizzle that had been falling all day. He pulled the hood up on his blue sweatshirt and tried to stay warm.

A case of beer sat at their feet in a soggy cardboard crate. Duane, who lived down the street and was one grade ahead of the others in school, had stolen the case from the back of a beer truck. On the way home from junior high he announced he'd sell the beers for a quarter apiece.

Willy handed Duane a dollar and picked out four cans, deliberating over which to choose as if one might be better than another. Mickey and Alan fished crumpled dollar bills from their pockets. Willy could still taste the pork chops and mashed potatoes his mother had served for dinner. He'd rushed through the meal and declined a second helping in order not to be late for the secret beer party. He'd told his mother he was going over to Mickey's house to play Ping-Pong. Mickey had told his own mother he was going to Willy's house to listen to records. Willy hoped the two mothers wouldn't be talking to each other on the telephone.

"Who's got a can opener?" Alan asked.

Suddenly there was panic and the prospect of a ruined evening. Then Duane started laughing.

"What's so funny?" Willy asked.

"All of you guys," Duane said. "Of course I got a can opener. How can you drink beer without a church key?" He stuck his hand inside his plaid flannel shirt and drew forth a can opener attached to a string around his neck. "This and a can of beer will get you into heaven," he laughed. "That's what my uncle says, the old fart."

They all relaxed.

"But heaven has a price," Duane continued, smiling a smile that irritated Willy. "It's going to cost a dime to open each beer."

Mickey and Alan grudgingly counted out their loose change, but Willy didn't have any more money. After much bickering Duane agreed to "loan" Willy the money necessary to open his beers, provided Willy paid Duane back as soon as he was able. Willy reluctantly agreed, and then to make himself feel better called Duane a scumbag.

With money already in his pocket, Duane could not be insulted. "So let's have a party," he said, slipping the can opener from around his neck and tossing it to Mickey. Mickey caught the opener and tossed it back again as though playing a game of hot potato. "You open the beer," Mickey said. "That's what we're paying you for."

Duane opened the beers and passed them around and the party began in earnest. Halfway through his second beer Duane wandered off to relieve himself. While he was gone Willy unzipped his fly and held his breath and ever so neatly pissed into Duane's beer can.

"What are you *doing?*" Mickey whispered.

"Paying Duane back," Willy said, trying to keep himself steady and not laugh. "You think this is about a dime's worth?"

6 · *Auto Repair*

Lydia had a crush on Willy.

"I don't know what to do," she told Vee.

"Why don't you call him."

They were in Lydia's bedroom, taking turns sipping from a bottle of crème de menthe Lydia had filched from the back of her father's liquor cabinet. Lydia's parents had driven to the city for the evening to have dinner and see a musical on Broadway. They'd be home late.

"I can't just *call* him, Vee," Lydia said. She took a sip from the bottle and rubbed her lips together. "Do you know what my mother told me? She told me I can't go out on a date at night until I'm sixteen." She made a face, then brightened. "But my father said if I get good grades this winter I can start whenever I'm ready. Isn't that sweet?"

Vee guessed that was pretty sweet and took another sip of crème de menthe, which was beginning to make her feel giddy. "Is my tongue as green as yours?" she asked Lydia.

They poked their tongues out at each other and compared. Lydia pulled a folded Kleenex from the back pocket of her jeans and tried to rub the green liqueur from her tongue, but the Kleenex stuck and came apart. Vee laughed.

"It's not funny," Lydia said. "And what should I do about Willy, anyway? You're not much help."

"I know," Vee said. "You've got to do something to impress him. That way you don't come right out and say you like him, you show him."

Lydia thought for a minute and then whispered, "What if we take my mother's Falcon and drive over to his house? That will impress him."

Vee didn't even bother to answer. Neither one of them had a license, let alone knew how to drive.

"It's an auto*ma*tic," Lydia said.

"Have you ever tried to drive before?"

"No, but my father told my mother any monkey on the block can drive an automatic. It should be fun, come on. You said yourself I ought to do something to impress Willy."

The red Falcon, which was parked in one bay of a two-car garage, started without a problem. Lydia flicked on the radio and then looked at herself in the rearview mirror. "My tongue's still green," she said. "I hope Willy doesn't notice." She put the car in reverse, but as she backed out she must have turned the wheel to the left, for the car emerged from the garage at a slight angle, enough for a loose strip of chrome on the passenger side to get snagged on the metal track of the overhead garage door. As the car continued in reverse the chrome strip curled back on itself like the skin of a banana being peeled.

"Stop!" Vee said.

Lydia jumped on the brake with both feet and the piece of chrome popped loose and clanked against the cement garage floor.

"What was *that*?" Lydia said.

"The chrome on the side of the car. I think you just knocked it off."

"Well it was on your *side*, Vee, you should have been watching for something like that."

Lydia pulled the Falcon back into the garage and the two girls got out and inspected the damage.

"My mother's going to kill me," Lydia said. "I know her, she'll go berserk. This kind of thing makes her crazy." Her face knotted and she looked as if she might cry. "I wonder if this happened because we took that bottle from my father's liquor cabinet. Do you believe in things like that? Do you think this happened because we did something we weren't supposed to do?"

Vee wasn't listening. She picked up the curled strip of chrome and tried to straighten it, but there were still creases all along its surface. She'd never thought about chrome before, how the strips were attached to the body of a car, but now she squatted down and followed with her eye the half-dozen metal clips fastened in a straight line to the car's side. "Maybe we can fix this ourselves," she said.

"But it's bent," Lydia said. "It's *wrinkled*. Even if you put it back again it's going to look sick." She took another folded Kleenex from the back pocket of her jeans and dabbed her eyes. Her plans were ruined, her mother would strangle her, she'd never be allowed to date at night for the rest of her life.

"But what if we get another one of these things?" Vee said. She stood and held the crooked chrome strip like a staff. "Half the people in our neighborhood have cars like this. You see them all over the place."

"I hardly think so," Lydia said. "I hardly think you know what you're talking about."

"Well *somebody* must have a Falcon. We'll just walk around the neighborhood until we find a car like your mother's."

"And then what?"

Vee bent over and held the creased strip of chrome against the side of the car. "Don't you see? This thing just snaps on and off. All we have to do is get another one." She went to the back of the garage, to the workbench where Lydia's father kept his tools. "There must be a screwdriver around here somewhere."

"Wait a minute," Lydia said. "I've got it, I've got it!" She jumped up and down and waved her closed hand, the one holding the damp Kleenex. "I've got a *brilliant* idea. I'll phone

Willy and explain what happened and tell him we just *have* to have his help."

"What do you want to do that for?" Vee said. She stared at Lydia from the dim light at the back of the garage. The crème de menthe had given her a headache. "You wrecked your mother's car, not Willy."

"I didn't *wreck* it, Vee, I just bent a little piece of metal. This is perfect, this solves all of our problems. Willy can find us another one of those metal strip things, and after he fixes the car he'll think he saved my life. Don't you see how perfect this is?"

Vee finally found a screwdriver, but after picking it up and holding it in her hand, she put it back down again.

7 · *Driven*

Willy stepped on the gas and the car jumped forward. When he hit sixty he eased his foot off the pedal and relaxed his grip on the wheel. The car belonged to his father and handled well, better than others he'd driven, though he was only seventeen and hadn't had much experience.

Matt lay in the backseat and urged Willy to drive faster. Whenever Matt felt the car decelerate he urged Willy to drive faster. That they might be approaching a bend in the road didn't matter. Willy could smell the bourbon on Matt and hoped his brother wasn't drunk enough to heave all over the backseat.

"Can't you go any faster?" Matt complained. "The road's empty."

He was right. You could lie in darkness in the backseat of a four-door sedan and just from what your ears told you know the road was wide and empty and still slick from a light snow that had fallen hours ago. Willy drove faster, but he was in no hurry. He knew what he was going to do with the evening.

The smell of bourbon sat in the car like a third passenger. Willy unrolled the window a crack and felt cool damp air pass over his hands and chill the steering wheel. He and Matt had spent the afternoon at a wedding. One of Matt's fraternity brothers from college had decided to get married during the

Thanksgiving recess. Fearing he might drink too much at the wedding and be unable to drive home, Matt had asked Willy to tag along.

After the ceremony at the church, all the guests were invited to a reception at the home of the bride's parents. Matt and his frat friends banded together and crowded the makeshift bar in the kitchen, growing more voluble and boisterous as they drank. At one point the groom, who sat at the kitchen table holding his bride in his lap, spilled a bottle of Beaujolais across the bodice of her wedding dress. She left the kitchen in tears and reappeared later in the company of her mother. The bride's father, meanwhile, had set up an auxiliary bar in the dining room and warned his older guests to avoid the kitchen.

Willy drank 7-Up and ate hors d'oeuvres that tasted like shrimp but had the consistency of soft cheese. Then he drank coffee and ate a piece of wedding cake and talked with the bride's relatives. Alcohol did not tempt him. After he and Matt had finally left the reception to make the twenty-five-mile drive back home, they stopped at a liquor store and Matt bought a pint of Jim Beam.

"Faster," Matt said from the backseat.

Willy stepped on the gas and hit eighty before easing off the pedal. He could hear bourbon sloshing against the pint bottle as Matt brought it to his lips, and then he felt the shock of cold glass as Matt pressed the bottle against the back of his neck.

"You want some?"

Willy didn't, his evening was planned and still in front of him, but to be a buddy he took the bottle and placed it between his legs, up tight next to his crotch, and held it for a while as he drove.

"I've got a date tonight," he said.

Willy didn't want to turn up at Christy's house with alcohol on his breath. Actually he didn't mind one way or the other, but Christy's parents minded terribly. The last time he'd picked her up he'd drunk a beer beforehand, an eighteen-ounce tallboy. He was nervous and the beer both relaxed him and gave him an edge he liked. Later he learned her father had smelled the beer on his breath. Christy's parents were old-fashioned—at least as old-fashioned as suburban people got. They went to the Methodist service every Sunday morning at nine and said grace before the evening meal. And they didn't drink. They didn't drink a drop. Christy warned Willy that if he showed up at her house with beer on his breath again her father would forbid her to see him.

Tonight would be the fourth time he'd taken Christy out. On their last date, after an hour-long campaign whose progress could be measured by the inch, Willy had been able to maneuver his hand beneath Christy's soft mohair sweater. Tonight he could begin with his hand beneath her sweater because Christy's chest was conquered territory. Her tits belonged to history. Tonight he wanted his hand beneath her pleated skirt, nestled between those magnetic thighs. On the following date he hoped to get *her* hand into *his* pants, and by the sixth date, if all went according to plan, Willy reasoned they could dispense with pants and skirts altogether. That was the moment he longed for, but to get to that point he'd have to be as patient as he was methodical.

He passed the bottle back to Matt, who sat up heavily and leaned forward in his seat with his arms on his knees and the bottle of bourbon wedged between both hands.

"Don't get mad," Matt said, "but I forgot to tell you something."

"Tell me what?" Willy kept his eyes on the road.

"You had a phone call before we left for the wedding. You were taking a shower, remember?"

"Sure I remember. Who called?"

"That girl you were going to see tonight. What's her name again?"

Willy looked at Matt in the rearview mirror. He could feel himself get mad, feel muscles tighten skin across his face. "Christy. Her name's Christy. What did she say?"

"She can't go out."

"Shit. What else?"

Matt took a swig from the bottle. "That she'll explain everything when she sees you in school on Monday. Sounded like problems with her father."

All day long Willy had been in a state of dreamy arousal. He stared at Matt in the mirror. Matt's sports coat was hitched up on his shoulders from when he'd been lying down.

"How could you forget something like that?" Willy asked.

"I don't know, I just forgot. We were in a hurry before we left and I forgot."

Matt passed the bottle over the front seat again. This time Willy took a long swallow before passing the bottle back. The bourbon burned his throat and made his eyes tear, but in no time at all his body felt warm and his limbs loose. He didn't say anything. His body felt good, but he was going to make himself stay mad. They were almost home, another three or four miles.

Then Matt asked, "Can't you go any faster?"

"I'm doing seventy-five and the road's wet," Willy said. "Why are you in such a hurry anyway? You're not going anywhere."

"Neither are you."

Willy looked in the rearview mirror and waited for Matt to take another drink. He waited, and the longer he waited the better he felt, as if by waiting, he was letting his anger ripen. When Matt finally brought the bottle to his lips, Willy punched the car's accelerator with his foot and bourbon came gushing out the neck of the bottle and splashed across Matt's chin and onto his shirt and jacket.

"Son of a bitch," Matt said.

8 · *The Party*

"Think of it as a drunken orgy," Vee told Willy in Spanish class. She was going to have a party the day they all graduated from high school.

Willy was impressed. "What about your parents? They don't mind?"

"They'll be on vacation. But they said I could have a few people over to the house to celebrate."

Willy laughed, knowing a few people might mean as many as fifty. He recalled afternoons hanging out at Vee's house with a circle of their friends. He recalled the den downstairs with the captain's chairs and prints of old sailing ships. He recalled the color TV and elaborate stereo, the bar against the back wall and the waxy linoleum floor perfect for dancing.

A big crowd turned out for the party, but by one in the morning only fifteen or twenty people remained. No one was entirely sober, and Vee's boyfriend, Tom, was further gone than the others. He was retelling his favorite story about the football player from a rival high school who'd been to a victory party with his teammates and gotten drunk. On a whim someone had handed him a fifth of vodka and dared him to chug it. The football player accepted the challenge and promptly drained the bottle, drained it dry like a true hero, a feat larger than life. But only fifteen seconds later he was unconscious, and when his teammates attempted to revive him, playfully at first but soon with alarm, they met with no success. Finally someone thought to check the football player's pulse. Zip, zero, c'est la vie. He was dead.

Nervous laughter followed Tom's story. Willy was behind the bar and had been mixing drinks for everyone for the last couple of hours. He felt wonderful, couldn't have felt better, though as a bartender he had his limitations. Gin and tonic was the drink he promoted, rum and Coke the alternate. Had anyone asked for a zombie or a Bombay bomber he would have been lost.

Just about then Tom stepped up to the bar and wondered, in a voice loud enough to unplug the party, if a bottle of vodka might be available. A couple in the corner stopped dancing, and then someone else took Wilson Pickett off the stereo. Willy guessed Tom was joking and rummaged beneath the bar until he found a bottle.

"So," Tom said, loud and cocky and swaying slightly, "who's got the balls to chug this bottle"—he wrinkled his brow to read the label—"to chug this bottle of Smirnoff's Vodka?"

No one said a word. Willy realized Tom wasn't clowning around and looked across the room, past the life buoy and decorative driftwood mounted on the wall, to see if anyone was witless enough to accept the challenge.

"I'll chug it," Vee said.

Naturally everyone thought she was kidding. Vee was a good student and would be attending art school in New York City in the fall. She was popular and attractive and had everything going for her. Everything, that is, except for Tom.

Tom was a problem. Football and lacrosse were his high school sports, and in both he excelled. But off the playing field he was always loud and full of bad air, and in the classroom he'd been hopelessly below average. During the school year Tom and Vee had made a handsome couple, but now that school was out Vee had qualms about being attached to a guy who had trouble reading labels on bottles. She'd confided as much to Willy, and she'd hinted to Tom they ought to see less of each other, but Tom hadn't gotten the message.

"I'll chug it," she said again.

"Hey Vee," Tom said, showing concern for the first time all evening, "I was talking to the guys."

Vee ignored him, throwing Tom further off balance. Finally he said, "If you want to chug it, babe, go ahead, you know what you're doing." But he looked unsettled and could hardly believe his own words.

Vee got behind the bar with Willy and he reluctantly handed her the bottle of vodka. "Stop screwing around," he whispered, but Vee ignored him too. She announced she'd need a minute to calm down and asked Willy for a cigarette. He'd only recently become a smoker and clumsily lit up for both of them, the cigarettes protruding from his mouth like cartoon fangs. Someone turned the stereo back on, and then someone else flicked on the color TV. Noise and busyness filled the den.

Vee appeared calm as she stubbed out her cigarette, but she couldn't have been calm, not inside, for she was about to do something daring. She and Willy talked behind the bar, but neither really listened to what the other said. Willy watched Vee's hands, which were now beneath the bar and talking a language of their own. Unscrewing the cap from the bottle, she emptied the vodka into the stainless-steel sink directly beneath the bar and then refilled the bottle with water from the tap. After replacing the cap she toweled the bottle dry and then stealthily put it back on top of the bar. None of her movements had been detected by anyone except Willy, and as she continued to talk it occurred to him that his function had been to serve as her decoy.

"All right everyone," Vee said. She held up the bottle for all to see and unscrewed the cap. Off again went the stereo and TV. The toilet in the hall flushed, and then there was silence.

Tom stood at the back of the room with his hands on his hips, a pose he normally assumed on the playing field. Heads turned from Vee to Tom and from Tom to Vee. Would he stop her? Willy was tempted to betray Vee's secret and disperse the crazy tension that charged the room. This was a party after all, what had been billed as a drunken orgy. But instead of saying anything he leaned against the bar and waited, with a straight face, like everyone else.

Vee brought the bottle to her lips and began to chug. People looked away as if she were tearing the legs from a frog. With the bottle half-empty Vee paused and there was a moment of silence you could have gotten lost in. She tilted the bottle back again and this time she finished it off. No one clapped or congratulated her. No one made a sound. They waited for her to pass out, to die. But she didn't pass out, she didn't even pretend to pass out. Instead, she walked steadily from behind the bar and across the room to where Tom stood.

"Why didn't you stop me?" she said. Tears ran from her face and made a mess of her mascara.

Tom looked as if he might hemorrhage his brain. He didn't answer Vee, his tongue was stuck, but a glimmering must have passed through him, and with it an understanding of where he suddenly stood with Vee, for all at once he was a blur of motion as he left the room. He couldn't get away fast enough.

Within minutes the party broke up. Some people were still under the impression Vee was drunk and perhaps very nearly dead, while others had guessed the deception. Willy stayed behind to help Vee clean up. Someone had been sick in the bathroom—a rum and Coke drinker by the look of it. Cigarette butts littered the linoleum floor, record albums without jackets were strewn across a couch.

"Hey Vee," Willy said a little later. They'd been making a sweep of the den to collect dozens of plastic glasses. Everyone else had gone home.

Vee looked up, once again calm and relaxed, though her cheeks were still streaked with mascara and her blonde hair was out of place.

"I was just wondering," Willy said, "if you were doing anything tomorrow night."

9 · *The Cure*

Turner was sitting still as death, his powers of concentration undaunted even in a place like the Blue Moon. Alone in the corner, he was seated at a round table covered with a red-and-white-checkered cloth. In front of him were three different bottles of imported beer. Also a pen and spiral notebook. When he finally drank from one of the bottles he rolled the beer around in the back of his mouth as if gargling, and as he did this you could see his Adam's apple dance up and down his throat. With pen in hand, poised just inches from the spiral notebook, he was ready to transfer deep sensation to paper. Then he heard, amid all the other noise and bluster in the Blue Moon, a lone hiccup.

Turner adjusted his glasses and looked up to see some guy standing at the bar and breathing into a brown paper bag. Every twenty or thirty seconds this guy hiccuped, bringing an amused grin to the bartender washing glasses in a sink of sudsless water behind the bar. Like many other people here, the bartender and Turner, as well as the guy hiccuping into the paper bag, were students.

Turner walked up to the bartender.

"Ritchie," he said, "cut me a wedge of lemon this big, and bring me a bottle of bitters."

While Ritchie the bartender and the now bagless student

with the hiccups looked on, Turner poured bitters over the wedge of lemon in the saucer, saturating the fruit as if marinating a piece of meat.

"What's your name?" Turner said to the hiccuping student, not looking up, his eyes intent on the confection he was preparing.

"Willy."

"That's terrific, Willy. Now do me a favor and suck on this." He brought the dripping wedge of lemon to within an inch of Willy's mouth. Willy accepted the wedge and screwed up his face, then spat the lemon violently into his palm as if dislodging a bone from his throat.

"Ritchie," Turner said flatly, ignoring Willy, "bring me a bowl of sugar, willya please."

Turner sprinkled sugar on the lemon like some kind of weary barroom paramedic. He was a graduate student and all of twenty-three. Willy was a nineteen-year-old sophomore. "Suck on it, Willy. Suck the juice and then eat the pulp."

Willy screwed up his face again. The dripping wedge of lemon, which now resembled a sticky and unappetizing piece of candy, was in his hand and beginning to dribble down his wrist. He hiccuped.

"Go ahead! You want to get rid of them or not?"

Willy did as he was told, and within a minute his hiccups had disappeared, vanished, gone to trouble someone else. He held out a hand for Turner to shake.

"Let me buy you a beer," he said.

Turner spent a lot of time at the Blue Moon, which was a big breezy place tricked out like a cowboy bar in turn-of-the-century Colorado. There was sawdust on the floor and a brass foot rail at the bar and a moose head with mange mounted to a plaque on the wall. But this was Boston, not Colorado, and the university was just two blocks away, so the Blue Moon, cowboy trappings aside, was more of a college bar than anything else. A great chrome and plastic jukebox that looked as if it might have been designed in Detroit spun the latest hits. There was a TV above the bar and Milton Glaser's poster of Dylan pinned to a door. And then there was the beer. The Blue Moon did beer in a big way. Beer from around the world. Harp, Stingo, Singha. Brahma and Hogshead and Peroni. Whitbread ale from London and Eagle lager from India. One hundred and eighty-seven brands in all. More beers than nations.

Turner was slowly compiling a taste list of all the beers the Blue Moon offered. When he drank at the bar he was working, and the compensation he received came in the form of free eats and beer and booze. Turner had already tasted and made notes on 119 different beers. He had 68 more to go, and when he finished he was going to turn the list over to the proprietor of the Blue Moon, who would make copies, like menus, to be kept at each table. Most of the beers just didn't move fast enough. The college kids came in and ordered Guinness stout or Heineken, and they thought they were stepping out. They thought they were adventuring. The proprietor wanted them to try other beers, like Sun Lik from Hong Kong or Monkey Meat from Djakarta. Two sixty-five a pop for those special brews. With Turner's taste list at each table, the proprietor figured all of the beers would move. He even had Turner assign a number to each beer. When a kid came in who couldn't even pronounce the name of one of the more exotic beers, no problem. Not to worry, sonny. Just give the waitress a number and nobody gets his feelings hurt.

The proprietor was taken with the taste list, and it wasn't even his idea. The idea belonged to Turner, who'd had an ulterior motive. Motives. Two of them. One, he'd been spending too much money drinking and figured there ought to be a way to drink for free. And two, Turner was studying to be a chemist. A *flavor* chemist. Someone who finds the chemical compounds that occur naturally in the fermentation process of beer. When he had completed the taste list he was going to submit a copy to one of his chemistry professors and receive three credits for it.

Willy was relieved to be rid of the hiccups, but he wasn't happy. He wasn't happy at all. Before wandering into the Blue Moon he'd taken a two-hour astronomy final, and before taking the final he'd spent twenty-four hours cramming for the exam in the library. In that time Willy had done absolutely nothing good for his body. He chain-drank coffee, smoked one cigarette after another, and ate cheese-flavored crackers that he bought from a vending machine in the basement of the library. Instead of sleep he made periodic trips to the bathroom and snorted crystal Methedrine up his nose through a plastic straw. Right now he needed food and sleep and a strong laxative. He could hear his nervous system buzzing insectlike in his ears, and after only half a bottle of beer he'd gotten the hiccups.

Willy told Turner about the astronomy final, complaining he had trouble studying in his dormitory because of the noise.

"You ought to find yourself a place off campus," Turner said matter-of-factly. "Split the cost with a roommate and it's not too bad."

Willy nodded, privately mulled the thought over.

"And think, no more cafeteria food. No more cold meat loaf or purple Jell-O. Eat what you want to eat." Turner paused and eyed Willy. "And when I say *eat*, I don't mean cheese-flavored crackers for Christ sake."

Turner then put away his spiral notebook and called out to Ritchie to bring over a bottle of Old Granddad and two shot glasses. He wanted to conduct a test. Willy needed an off-campus apartment, Turner had one. Turner needed a roommate, Willy was available. But first, Turner wanted to see whether Willy would be a compatible drinking partner. That would make things so much easier. Turner had already run through two roommates this semester alone. He just couldn't hang on to anybody. They all thought him peculiar, a Jekyll-

and-Hyde personality, which in fact was true. Turner had the highest grade point average in his graduate department. He studied rigorously and never missed a lecture or lab, but when he wasn't studying or going to class he was drinking himself into a stupor. No one knew how he did it, how he could drink and carry on like a bum and get the grades of a whiz kid.

As Turner and Willy sipped one shot after another, Turner's fears about Willy were allayed and he had a chicken club sandwich brought to the table. "Eat," he said. "Eat before you die on me for Christ sake."

Willy woke to the sound of clinking glass. He was lying on a bare mattress and still had his clothes on, even his shoes, which were damp and gave off an unpleasant animal odor. His throat was dry and his head felt swollen, as if he'd soaked his brain in a bucket all night. Sun poured in through a window without curtain. Willy turned over and faced a blank white wall, faced oblivion, whatever was or wasn't there, and tried to fall back to sleep. But then he heard more clinking, more of that nerve-racking glass on glass, like an endless round of toasts.

With a sudden racing of the heart he remembered where he was—Turner's apartment, half of which was now his. He remembered scribbling out a check to Turner for two months' rent. He remembered they stopped by his room at the dormitory and cleared out what the two of them could carry—textbooks, a duffel bag stuffed with clothes, a wooden crate holding record albums, and then another box containing notebooks and paperbacks and a portable radio. How had they carried all of that stuff?

Willy crawled out of bed head first, thinking of the lizards behind glass partitions in the reptile house at the city zoo. His body smelled fetid, his skin felt greasy. He tried lifting the crate of record albums and groaned. Then he heard that sound again, that infernal clinking.

Turner had lined up in a neat row a dozen different glass

containers of vitamins and minerals, making a terrible racket on the Formica kitchen table. There were ten oranges on the table as well, all halved, five of them already squeezed dry of juice. A Styrofoam carton of eggs peeked out from behind the row of vitamins and minerals.

"Good morning," Turner said brightly. "You look sick, my boy. You look like a piece of diseased meat."

Willy said nothing. His eyes were squinted, his face puffy.

"It's noon, Willy. Rise and shine."

Turner himself had already been up for an hour. He'd shaved and showered and was now comfortably wrapped in a terry-cloth bathrobe and an old pair of moccasins. The thick lenses of his glasses gleamed.

"Don't you have a hangover?" Willy asked. He found a mangled pack of cigarettes—he'd slept on the pack—in his shirt pocket, and lit a bent cigarette on the front burner of the stove. "Shit," he said quietly, more to himself than to Turner, "I still have another final on Monday. Restoration drama. I've got to read six plays between now and then."

Turner sighed. "Willy, *I've* got another final on Monday too. The whole goddamn *university* has finals on Monday. Do you think I'm going to let a little drunk get in the way of my studies?"

"A big drunk, Turner."

"All right, a big drunk. But there are things you can do to ease the pain. Use your head, my boy. First of all, you can write off studying for today. Nothing good will come of it, I know. Second, you can start following my regimen. I've got a *cure* for hangovers, Willy."

Willy looked doubtful, even suspicious.

"See this?" Turner's arm swept grandly above the kitchen table. "Fresh orange juice. I've already had mine, these five round beauties are for you. You get your vitamin C from the juice. Next, we stir two raw eggs in with the OJ. That's your cysteine, which is an amino acid. Very important. Can't live without it. Almost half a gram in those two eggs. Drink this concoction and you're going to feel better."

Willy made a face.

"Don't fuck with chemistry, Willy! I know what I'm doing, believe me. Did I get rid of your hiccups or not?"

Willy contrite.

"You bet I did. Now if you take these with the juice"—he pointed to the containers of pills—"two things are going to happen. One, in a little while you're going to feel almost normal, despite all the drinking we did last night. And two, you'll put *back* all those nutrients the alcohol robbed from you while you were drunk. It's like a stickup, Willy. Last night you were mugged, and this morning you're doing the right thing and going to the cops. You're going to get back your property, what's owed you. You're going to straighten this whole mess out."

"I don't know, Turner. I'm not even sure what all this stuff is."

"It's the stuff of life for Christ sake! You wanna be a stupid drunk or a smart one? This"—again he pointed—"is vitamin A. Then there's B-one, B-two, niacin, B-five, B-six, B-twelve, and E. These last two here, the chelated zinc and the selenium, are minerals. You need them all."

"Turner, all I need is a cup of coffee and a hot shower. And while we're at it, I could do without you in my face."

"Fine! Smoke your cigarettes and drink pots of coffee and make yourself feel even worse. Tobacco and coffee *suck the C* right out of you. You some kind of moron for Christ sake? You some kind of monkey that swings from a vine? It's going to be two days before you're back to normal and you've got the right balance of nutrients again. But go ahead, you know best. Asshole! Asshole in a brown paper bag, that's you. Cheese crackers and crystal Meth, probably *bad* crystal Meth, probably cut with Drano, there's a modern remedy. Kill yourself quickly, I don't care. I just met you yesterday, and here I am trying to save your life."

"You're trying to hang on to a roommate, so cut the crap." Willy looked around the kitchen for an ashtray, but there wasn't one in sight. Finally he flicked his cigarette butt into the kitchen sink, a ten-foot shot that hit with a satisfying hiss. The apartment was half his now.

"And while you're drinking coffee and pissing away what's left of your body's immune system," Turner continued, "I'm going to go out and get a light breakfast. How does a fresh bran muffin and a cup of tea sound to you? I know, probably too healthy. Well tough shit. And this afternoon, while you're going to hell in a hung over body full of toxins, I'll take a nap and maybe watch the Celtics on the tube. *That's* part of the hangover cure too, don't you know. Relaxation, Willy. Sensible rest. Give your poisoned body a break, if you follow me. Tonight I'll have a drink or two and a hot dinner and go to bed early."

Willy needed aspirin. Right away. A handful of extrastrength something.

"And tomorrow morning," Turner was saying, "stay out of my way. I don't wanna hear a goddamn peep out of you. Tomorrow is study day, with breaks for food and exercise—"

"Okay, okay," Willy said, pointing to the smorgasbord of vitamins and minerals, raw eggs and fresh juice. "I'll give your cure a try. I can't feel any worse than I already do. But Jesus, Turner, I've got to say this right now, right out front. You're a very strange guy."

Turner smiled broadly, showing his white teeth and healthy pink gums. "You bet I am," he said. "And some day you'll appreciate the fact. Some day you're going to miss your Turner."

10 · *Hives*

"You know what I think?" Melinda said.

Vee was on her stomach in her own bed, a pillow pulled over her head, but she could still hear the sound of Melinda's voice.

"I think you spend too much time by yourself. You ought to get out some."

What about you? Vee thought. You and Benny never leave the room. She turned on her side and tried to will herself to sleep. The girls' beds were separated by a night table built into the wall.

"Maybe Benny could set you up with one of his friends. You want me to speak to Benny?"

Vee lay still, but silently she said no, don't speak to Benny, don't speak to anybody, especially me and especially now, I want to *sleep*. Surely it was after midnight.

When Vee was a child her bedroom had been a haven, a place filled with stillness, a room never shared. All of that changed when she went away to college and lived in a dormitory where roommates were assigned and the luck of the draw prevailed. Melinda came from Oklahoma, from a family of four children, and had always bunked at home with her younger sister. A chronic chatterbox, Melinda wound the day down with a good talk before drifting off to sleep. Drifting off, as it turned out, often took as long as an hour or two. Vee tried to discourage Melinda by simply not responding, but this rarely worked. Melinda didn't require conversation, merely another presence.

"I'm not sure it's altogether healthy," Melinda was saying. "A girl on her own so much, without company to keep. We all have urges, Vee." She laughed to herself. "Just ask Benny."

Vee wanted to laugh too, but for another reason. She'd once tried to imagine Benny without clothes, but couldn't get past his large outer bulk and dark eyes like bits of polished plastic, a teddy bear dressed in boots and wrinkled western wear. She wondered if there would be a penis beneath the faded jeans.

"Vee," Melinda said. "I know you're not asleep. You can't fool me. I can't be fooled, honey. Don't you ever get lonely? I'm concerned about you. I seriously am. You're either here or over in that fine arts building, one place or the other. You ought to get out just a bit, find a guy, find yourself a Benny. And then you watch what happens. If he's a Benny there'll be glue between the two of you. You'll never want to leave his room."

Vee opened her eyes, feeling her lashes bat against the pillow case. *His room?* she thought.

Melinda and Benny found each other two weeks into the fall semester. They dated once, draft beer and a set of country music at the Lone Star Café, and from that night forward behaved as if they were childhood sweethearts. Benny was a second-year music major who studied composition and played the piano and guitar. He lived off campus, over in the East Village in a tenement on Avenue C, with three other university students. The four of them shared a two-bedroom apartment with mattresses on the floor and the sound of rats scampering between the walls.

Some days Benny could be seen in a "Save The Armadillos" T-shirt and a pair of aviator sunglasses. The sunglasses looked out of character—too sinister for a twenty-year-old with such a large round face and curly helmet of hair—but the folksiness of the T-shirt somehow fit. Benny had been born in Arizona but had grown up in northern California, along the coast, one of those towns famous not for its beaches but its scenic bluffs. He once told Vee he missed the ocean.

"You mean the Pacific?" Vee said.

"Yeah, the ocean."

"There's another ocean about a mile from here," she joked. "We call it the Atlantic."

Benny laughed easily, as much at himself as anything else. And Vee kind of liked Benny, too—his genial nature and his way with a guitar, the hand-tooled cowboy boots and the hokey leather belt with the big brass buckle.

But for all of that Benny had one exasperating habit. Men were allowed in the women's dormitories from twelve noon until nine in the evening. Benny would show up at Vee and Melinda's room early in the afternoon, usually with his guitar, and some days he'd still be there at curfew, six or seven hours later. He was always around. He and Melinda would study and read, would sit cross-legged on the bed while Benny picked a song out of the air. They'd listen to the stereo, listen to news and endless talk on Melinda's clock radio while snacking from an open bag of corn chips, keeping to the room as if grazing in a fenced-off field. From her desk Vee would hear sweet romantic nonsense passing from one mouth to the other. She'd hear the groan of Melinda's mattress and the squeak of springs and turn to see the two of them locked in deep embrace yet fully dressed, Benny still wearing his boots.

Other than attending class or going out to eat, they hardly went anywhere at all. Vee understood this couldn't be strictly true, Benny was in a Bluegrass band and spoke of practicing with his group, though when he found time for this Vee could only guess. The two of them always seemed to be within the sound of each other's whisper, close enough to touch or tickle, using Melinda's bed as an all-purpose desk and love nest. Vee herself was dating no one at the time and felt uneasy sitting in on Melinda and Benny's intimacy. Melinda even had an extra key made in case Benny wanted to drop by and she wasn't around. Refuge for Vee wasn't possible. And if Benny stayed an hour or two beyond curfew, which happened, which happened with increasing frequency, he simply slipped out the window boots first and disappeared in the dark. With the room on the ground floor, the setup was nothing if not convenient.

At least their class schedules were different. While Vee studied fine arts, Melinda planned to major in either political science or journalism. The gossipy side of politics intrigued her—corrupt and venal officials, dirty tricks, the sexual misconduct of congressmen. She read the New York and Washington papers and never failed to watch the network news programs, always alert for scandal in high places.

These enthusiasms were not shared by Vee.

Another night, lights out, the girls in their respective beds. Benny had only recently made good his escape, nearly three hours after curfew this time. Vee was peeved.

"Well can you blame him for hanging around so?" Melinda said. "You ought to see the rat hole he lives in. My God, this city. Somebody ought to blow the whistle on the slumbucket that owns the building. Just be happy you don't live over there."

"But that's what I mean," Vee said. "*We* live over here and *Benny* lives over there. If he wants to visit he can visit, I'm all for visits, just not all the time. This is our place, not his. I can't even change my clothes without having to go down the hall to the bathroom."

Melinda sat up in the dark. "Is that what you're all bothered about? I'd never have taken you for such a prude, Vee."

This was hardly the reply Vee had expected. This wasn't what she was getting at. When she went to the beach in the summer she wore a bikini and didn't worry how much of herself was showing. She liked the sun, she liked browning her body. If you wanted a tan, you wore as little as you could get away with. Why had Melinda called her a prude? In high school, she'd played around with her boyfriend Tom, and not just once, many times, maybe too many times, a collection of beds that included an inflatable raft in a backyard pool and the last row of a movie theater.

"Just tell Benny not to hang around so much," Vee said.

"Or what?"

"I want you to let Benny know."

"What will happen, honey? Will you run to Mrs. C. and tattle on us?"

Every dormitory had its housemother. Vee had met this particular woman on the first day of school. Mrs. C. was polite but kept her distance. She could be seen coming and going, but never standing still and talking with the girls or watching television in the lounge off of the central foyer. As far as Vee was concerned, Mrs. C. lived in the shadows, a background figure hardly there at all, though technically she was the law. Going to her was like dialing 911.

"Come on, Vee, tell me what will happen."

"I don't *know* what will happen. I just know I'm getting sick of the situation, Melinda."

"Well you're in luck, sweetie, because there's an old remedy we practice on the prairie. It's called suck a rock."

Terrific, Vee thought, each remark gets more abusive than the last. "Just be sure to tell Benny, all right?" She took a breath and went on. "And by the way, the next time the two of you make love on your bed there, try doing it without your clothes on for once. It's more fun that way, trust me."

End of argument, nothing resolved. Melinda had run out of words, but still Vee couldn't sleep.

After lunch she checked her mail slot in the dorm foyer and found a note urging her to appear that evening at eight in Mrs. C.'s room. A bottle of gin, the note said, had been found on the top shelf of her closet. Alcohol was a forbidden substance in the dormitories. The possession of alcohol could get you expelled, at least according to university bylaws written way back when.

Vee reread Mrs. C.'s note and tried to laugh, tried to spot the gag between the lines, but she only found herself getting mad. She didn't keep gin in her closet or anywhere else, and even if she did, how serious was the crime? An art student she knew was shooting heroin before morning classes and still managing to get A's. Marijuana and mescaline could be bought in the student union building, angel dust over on First Avenue. Drinking alcohol was almost a retrograde activity.

Obviously someone had planted the bottle, and the who and why of it were not very difficult to figure. Vee could always deny the gin was hers, but then Mrs. C. would ask for an explanation. If the bottle wasn't Vee's, who did it belong to and how did it get in her closet? They were all friends here, all students. Mrs. C. herself was a student, in fact had been a student ever since she'd been hired as a housemother seven years earlier. Now she was finishing her master's and making plans for her doctorate. In another two or three years she'd be qualified to teach. And why, she would again inquire of Vee, should anyone want to hide a bottle of gin in your closet and cause you trouble?

Vee sat in the dorm lounge off of the foyer, Mrs. C.'s note in hand. A few girls between classes were watching television, a soap opera situated in a hospital. One girl drank from a can of diet cola, another stirred a cup of pineapple yogurt with a plastic spoon. Vee began to think she might go a step beyond protest and denial and try to prove the bottle wasn't hers. She looked again at the girl eating yogurt in front of the television screen.

When Vee was small, maybe seven or eight years old, she'd eaten a fresh piece of pineapple heavy with juice, the smell of it like a tropical perfume, and twenty minutes later her face and neck broke out in hives and she was sobbing in front of a mirror. An allergist later told her parents Vee was antipathetic to the fruit. Nothing dangerous, he said, just a low-grade allergy, a day's discomfort, but all the same it was best to avoid pineapple or any pineapple by-products.

Vee thought of the bottle of gin as she stared from the corner of her eye at the girl eating yogurt. She didn't even know what brand she was supposed to have been drinking, but maybe that didn't matter.

A few minutes before meeting Mrs. C. that evening, Vee spooned up the last bits of Dole's Crushed Pineapple from a six-ounce can. Mrs. C. had the gin bottle in her room. Vee's plan was to demonstrate the bottle couldn't have been hers by taking a drink in front of the housemother. "You see," she would say as hives began mapping her face, "I've always been allergic to alcohol. Why in the world would I keep a bottle of gin in my closet?"

Mrs. C. was waiting in her room when Vee knocked at the door and entered. She was shown an armchair across from the sofa where Mrs. C. sat, hands in her lap. Other than a garnet birthstone ring, Mrs. C. wore no jewelry. Between the armchair and sofa was a lacquered end table, and on top of the table stood the half-empty fifth of gin—Gilbey's in a frosted glass bottle.

"I want you to know I don't approve of snitching," Mrs. C. began. "I don't like the way this bottle came to my attention."

Vee nodded solemnly and felt herself fill with hope. Surely Melinda had already damaged herself through a clumsy act of informing. Directly above Mrs. C.'s head was a wall clock mounted in a stylized brass fixture that depicted the sun's golden rays. Vee was able to look at Mrs. C. and the clock on the wall at the same time. Her scalp was beginning to tingle. In just a few minutes her face and neck would flash and swell in odd red patches and she'd be wearing the proof she needed, provided she got to the gin first.

"Be that as it may," Mrs. C. said, "this bottle was found in your closet. We can't get around the fact. I'm sure you know. . . ."

Vee nodded again, but she'd already begun edging away from what was being said. Her wish was for a glass and the opportunity to roll smoothly into the gin demonstration.

"Only a few years ago," Mrs. C. was saying, "we wouldn't have even been having this conversation. You would have been in the dean's office with your parents, and who knows what might have come of it. Well we don't work that way anymore, thank you. Times have changed, we're a little more permissive. New York is a very sophisticated place. We can't expect students to be oblivious to what goes on all around them." Mrs. C. allowed herself a small smile here, though what the smile signified eluded Vee.

"Whenever a disciplinary problem of this sort comes up now, I decide what should be done. The dean has given me that authority. All housemothers have that authority."

Vee looked at the clock on the wall, only to be diverted when Mrs. C. lifted the bottle of gin from the end table.

"This bottle represents more than one evening's foolishness," she said. "How do I know this? Because the bottle's half-full. Somebody's been drinking, and somebody plans to drink again."

Vee scratched at a spot just below her ear. She'd taken off her earrings for fear her earlobes would swell. "Mrs. C.," she said.

"Let me finish, Vee. You'll have your turn in just a minute. I want you to understand I don't take any of this lightly, all right? I honestly don't know whether this bottle is yours or not, and I won't know until you tell me. Listen to me. I'm going to trust you. Whatever you say I'll abide by, I'll believe, that's how I am. You're going to be your own judge."

"All right," Vee said. She leaned forward, wondering where a glass might be found. She didn't want to drink straight from the bottle. "Mrs. C.," she said.

"Just a minute, I'm not quite through. Before you say anything, I want to explain the consequences of your decision. If you tell me the gin doesn't belong to you, nothing will happen. Do you understand? It's that simple. Nothing happens."

Vee said yes, she understood.

"But if you tell me you've been foolish, then I'll have to take the necessary steps to see this doesn't happen again. On the other side of my apartment," she said, waving her arm at the wall behind her, "is an empty room, a single. No one lives there. No yet, anyway. But every term there's always some girl who gets herself into trouble. Maybe it's boy trouble, maybe it's drinking or drugs, but it never fails, somebody always goes too far. When that happens I take the girl out of the double she's been sharing with her roommate, and I put her in the single next door to me where I can keep an eye on her. This was the dean's idea. It's been very effective the last several years." Here Mrs. C. allowed another smile to break the set of her mouth. "No one gets expelled these days," she confided, "they just get a little more attention."

Vee had been attending more to the sound of Mrs. C.'s voice than to the words she was speaking, waiting for a break in speech, a place she could slip through to begin her demonstration. Her face needed scratching. What exactly had been said, anyway? A single room was available? If she admitted the bottle was hers she'd be reassigned a room of her own? A room in which to do some kind of penance and prove she could be good? Was that it? There would be no more Benny? No Melinda?

Vee said nothing. If she moved into a single, Melinda would get the double all to herself and have Benny late into the night. That's what she wanted, and that didn't sound so good. But what did Vee want? There was actually a choice. She could have a room to herself by feigning guilt, or she could keep her room with Melinda. If Vee chose to detail the Benny/Melinda problem in high relief, if she set Mrs. C. straight, Benny would surely have his visiting privileges permanently revoked. One way or another, Benny would be gone, he'd be a ghost. But what about Melinda? She'd be worse than ever, just a bitch to live with.

"What's the matter?" Mrs. C. was suddenly saying. Her hand was pressed to her cheek, her garnet ring catching the light and playing off the ceiling.

Vee stared blankly back at Mrs. C.

"Your face, dear."

Vee put her hand to her forehead and felt the first welting of skin, hive number one, just above her eyebrow. In another minute her face and neck would be pulsing red, wheals turning her smooth skin coarse and ugly. In another five minutes she'd look like someone in need of professional care. She thought fast and said, "I'm upset."

Mrs. C. stared in mute wonder, stiff as a block of carved stone.

Vee thought it might be appropriate to demonstrate her agitation, demonstrate *something,* she'd been thinking in terms of demonstration half the day, but once again she felt herself fill with hope, the feeling almost physical, almost erotic. By embracing guilt she could have her own room.

"I'm so upset," she said again, "but I'll be all right. This happens whenever I get nervous. Some girls cry, I break out in hives."

The simplicity of the explanation seemed to relieve Mrs. C., though her hand was still pressed to her cheek.

"But I feel bad," Vee said. "In fact I feel rotten. I think it's time I told you the truth." Her eyes went from Mrs. C. to the frosted bottle of Gilbey's on the lacquered end table. "At first I thought just one drink before bed might help me sleep. . . ."

11 · *Hard Luck*

Early one Saturday afternoon.

While Turner studied a chemistry text in the rocker and sipped bouillon from a mug, Willy stretched out on the cot they used as a sofa and read a novel. The radio was playing faintly, a classical station, when an announcer interrupted with a weather bulletin.

Willy looked up from his book. "Blizzard?" He went over to the living-room window. Snow was already falling. "I've got a date this evening," he said.

Turner joined Willy at the window. "Forget your precious date. I have a ticket to see the Bruins play at the Garden. I've been looking forward to this game all week, goddamn it."

By five o'clock there were eleven inches of snow on the ground. Turner had been listening intently to the radio ever since the first bulletin. When the hockey game was canceled, he started drinking.

"Admit defeat," he said to Willy from the rocker. "Might as well cut your losses and crack a beer."

Willy was peering out the window again, watching a snow-plow work its way up the street. "We were going to get a drink at the Blue Moon," he said, "then try this new Italian place. Seemed like a good choice for a second date."

"I'm telling you the whole city's shutting down. If the Bruins don't play, no one plays, including you. Give your genitals the night off."

Willy ignored Turner and began sifting through his wallet. When he found the slip of paper with Lila's name on it, he dialed her number and invited her to dinner at the apartment. "See you about eight," he said. With a one-minute phone call he'd salvaged the evening.

Turner was appalled. "What have you done? You're asking the poor girl to drive over here in a blizzard? Are you out of your mind?"

"She lives in the building," Willy said. He pointed to the ceiling. "Fourth floor. We met downstairs in the laundry room. Fun underwear."

"Christ," Turner said. He went to the refrigerator for another beer. "Why did you have to invite her to dinner? You know I don't like strange company."

"She's not strange company, she's a student like half the other people in this building. You want to join us for dinner?"

"Now I'm trapped," Turner was saying. "Now I'll have to hide out in my room." He paused. "Or will I?"

"What's that?"

"Have you given any thought to what you're going to serve this fun friend of yours?" Turner rubbed his hands together. "I think we can scare up some Campbell's Cream of Mushroom, but if you want something with a little texture to it, something you can *chew*, I'm afraid you're out of luck."

"I'll go to the store," Willy said. "It's only three blocks."

"In this weather? Have you been snorting crystal Meth again? I've told you, they're shutting the city down."

Willy put on his parka and boots, began wrapping a scarf around his neck. "How are we on liquor?" he said.

Turner stopped rocking. "Oh Jesus, I'm getting as bad as you. Where have I been? I don't think we've got but half a bottle of bourbon. We're in the middle of a blizzard and we don't have provisions."

"Let's hope the stores haven't closed early," Willy said.

"Not the liquor stores. They'll be jammed to the last minute, I promise you. They'll be doing banner business in this kind of weather. People stock up during disasters."

Willy returned before Turner and unpacked groceries. He was going to make spaghetti with sweet Italian sausage. He dug out pots and pans, a ladle and colander and sharp knife, and began chopping onions and green bell peppers for the sauce.

Turner finally arrived with a large snow-covered box in his hands. "Seventeen inches and still falling," he said. "I took a reading."

Willy eyed the box. "What did you get? All we needed was another bottle."

"You're not thinking, Willy. It's *bad* out there. Even the Bruins called it quits, and ice is their *medium*. We could be holed up for days."

"How much did you spend?"

"Emergency preparedness doesn't come cheap. You'll thank me later. Fortunately the liquor store had the good sense to take my personal check. Now what have we here?" He hoisted two cases of beer from the box. "One for you and one for me, fair and square. What else? Why here's a quart of Old Granddad for Willy, and, *and*, a quart of same for Turner. Aren't we democratic."

"I think what we are is pretty well set," Willy said, stirring his sauce with a wooden spoon.

"Not quite, my boy." He lifted a third bottle from the box, different from the other two. "Any financial planner will tell you that without a reserve fund you're sunk." He held up a bottle of Chivas Regal long enough for Willy to see the label, then put it in the cabinet above the sink, next to the glasses.

"I just hope to God we don't have to tap that baby," he said.

Willy's tomato sauce was simmering when Lila arrived a little after eight. Turner had long since retreated to his own room, a tumbler of bourbon in hand. Before sitting down to eat, Willy and Lila knocked at his door with a plate of spaghetti and sweet sausage.

"Come in," Turner said. He was seated in front of an open window, wearing his pea jacket and woolen watch cap. A six-pack was chilling on the ledge.

"Twenty-three inches and no end in sight," he said to Lila by way of introduction. "I don't know if Willy has told you, but I'm taking readings for one of the TV stations. I've got to stay by my post. Thanks for the spaghetti. You kids go and enjoy yourselves."

After dinner Willy made drinks, cut the lights, and curled up next to Lila on the cot. The television was tuned to a Robert Mitchum movie. Things are proceeding nicely, Willy thought, sipping his bourbon on the rocks. But before the first commercial break, Turner was in the middle of the living room and the lights were blazing.

"Who wants to play hockey?" he said. He went to his room and came back dragging a Masonite rink four feet long and nearly three feet wide. "Here's a stick for Lila, a stick for Willy, and the Bobby Orr autographed model for me." He set the rink up on the floor.

Lila turned to Willy for an explanation.

"Knock hockey," Willy said. "A very simple game. You take your stick and you hit the wooden puck, the object being to get the puck into your opponent's net at the end of the board there. Players take turns with their shots. That's all there is to it."

"Don't let him fool you," Turner said. "It may sound simple, Lila, but to play the game well requires a keener standard of precision than some people can muster. I hope you've been lifting weights lately. Now who would you like to be? What team?"

She looked at Willy. "The Los Angeles Dodgers?" She'd grown up in Orange County, was accustomed to ice in plastic trays.

"Willy, tell her we're playing hockey, not baseball."

"She can be whoever she wants," Willy said.

"Fine, fine, as long as I'm the Bruins there won't be a contest anyway. How about you, Willy? Pick a team."

Willy held his miniature hockey stick like a guitar and began strumming. "The Rolling Stones," he said. "I'm going to have Jagger facing off and Charlie Watts guarding the net."

"Christ, what have I gotten myself into? Lila, love, would you be a dear and pass me that bottle of Old Granddad?"

The games were short and permitted everyone a chance to play. Two teams competed while the third refereed. The first team to score three goals got to stay on the ice. At the end of each game the ref became the challenger.

The Bruins, not surprisingly, took an early lead in the series, but the Stones soon caught up. With each victory Turner or Willy downed a shot of bourbon, making the outcome of the series all but inevitable. If they played long enough the Dodgers would skate away with the cup.

Only when Turner's stick began flying out of his hand with every slap shot, well after midnight, was he willing to concede.

"The Bruins are the best type of losers," he told Lila, "which means they get sore as hell when they don't win. I want a rematch at your earliest convenience." And then he crawled up onto the cot and began snoring. Willy draped a blanket over Turner's shoulders and withdrew with Lila to his own room.

He had a secret reserve fund of his own. In the bottom drawer of his dresser was an unopened bottle of Courvoisier his brother Matt had given him for his last birthday. Willy uncorked the bottle and headed back to the kitchen to get a couple of glasses.

"Why don't you put a record on?" he said.

"What about Turner?"

"He's out cold. Be right back."

Willy hadn't been gone more than ten or fifteen seconds when Lila heard a violent smashing of glass. She ran to the kitchen.

"Turner's reserve," Willy said, looking sheepish.

"I don't understand."

"I knocked a full bottle of Chivas into the sink when I reached for a glass. Should have put the damn light on. The bottle just exploded when it hit. There's broken glass all over the place."

"I'll help you clean it up," Lila said.

"No, I'll do it in the morning, let's not worry about it now."

"Are you sure?" She walked over to Willy, glass crunching beneath her shoes, and put a hand on the back of his neck. Not until the next day would Willy realize just how drunk they had all become.

"Yeah, I'm sure," he said. "Come on."

Turner had slept through the crash, and he continued to sleep with the stereo blasting from Willy's bedroom. So far so good, Willy thought, but now something else was wrong. While he danced to the drum-happy rock and roll and lurched about the room, Lila sat on the corner of his bed and said nothing. For the first time all evening she appeared uncomfortable.

"What's the matter?" Willy asked her.

Lila looked below her waist to the tight wraparound skirt she was wearing, which ran to mid-calf. She'd made the skirt herself. She made most of her clothes.

"I should have worn pants," she said. "I can't dance in this thing."

Willy smiled like a wolf, which is to say he smiled to himself, from the inside. "If you take off your skirt," he said, "you can wear *my* pants." He beamed at Lila from across the room.

While Willy took off his jeans, Lila unwrapped what seemed like yards of fabric and let her skirt fall to the floor. Willy upped the ante and continued to strip, taking off his socks and then his vest and shirt. Lila followed suit and pulled her sweater over her head. She smiled coyly, and with good reason. She wasn't wearing a bra.

Drunk and dizzy with a moment that doesn't come often enough, the two of them stood in the middle of the floor and stared at each other, Willy in his jockey shorts and Lila wearing nothing but a pair of black nylon panties with a red heart appliquéd to the crotch. Fun underwear.

Dancing now seemed an exercise without point. Taking the bottle of Courvoisier with them, Willy and Lila sat cross-legged on Willy's bed and talked and drank and brazenly eyed each other. Soon enough the obvious occurred and they began to kiss and fondle, but to Willy's chagrin he discovered he couldn't get an erection. This had never happened to him before.

Maybe I'm just nervous, he thought. He told Lila to lie on her back and peeled off her black panties with the red heart and began playing with her, first with his fingers and then with his tongue. Lila's pubic hair was neatly trimmed to a narrow and furry black stripe. She responded to Willy's touch by arching her back and moaning into a pillow. She was real slippery down there.

But despite Lila's excitement Willy still wasn't hard. Finally he admitted he was too drunk to continue and they simply held each other. A minute later he passed out.

He woke with a parched throat and an aching head and a hard-on sent from heaven. He thought of the hard-on as a gift and wondered whether any other men in Boston had been similarly blessed this morning.

Lila was already awake and sitting up in bed, the sheet and blanket pulled to her midriff and her breasts looking even more shapely in the light of day than Willy had remembered from the night before. She read from one of the magazines that had been on his night table. She didn't yet know that he had awakened.

Willy smiled to himself and stared at Lila's breasts and tried to memorize with his eyes the size and shape of her nipples. A woman's nipples always surprised him. Finally, he thought, finally I'm going to get a chance to pounce on this splendid-looking lady. But first he needed something for his dry throat.

Willy kissed Lila good morning, excused himself, and rolled out of bed as if he were a dancer taking the stage. He didn't care if he had a hangover. He walked to the kitchen naked, his magnificent hard-on prominently on display. Seconds later he was swearing with a vengeance.

Lila yanked the top sheet from the bed and threw it over her body. Turner had beaten her to the kitchen and was already helping Willy stretch out on his back on top of the Formica table. There was blood all over the kitchen floor. "Down, boy, down," Turner was saying. Only now was Willy's erection beginning to subside.

"What happened?" Lila said.

Willy tried to laugh. "Remember that bottle I dropped last night?"

Turner interrupted. "Willy thought he'd use his foot as a broom. That sheet you're wearing, Lila, I need it, quick."

She offered no resistance as he grabbed an edge and pulled the sheet from her body. He worked very fast, ripping the sheet into long strips. Despite the jokes and bizarre behavior, Turner knew exactly what he was doing. He folded the last strip quickly but neatly and applied it to Willy's heel with the palm of his hand.

"I'll need pillows to keep the leg elevated," he said, "and a blanket for Willy. And for Christ sake, put some clothes on. This isn't the Playboy mansion."

When Lila returned she spread a blanket over Willy's chest and thighs and placed two pillows beneath his leg. She was wearing one of his shirts and the black panties with the red heart.

"A nasty gash," Turner was saying. "Four inches in length if my reading is right. Depth of laceration as yet undetermined. When the bleeding stops we'll clean the heel and do some probing, see if there's any glass still in there. It's a good thing you stepped where you did, Willy. If that had been your instep, we'd have had a severed artery to contend with. Arterial reconstruction is not my specialty, though I suppose I could have given it a go."

"What about a doctor?" Willy said. He found himself gritting his teeth. The heel was beginning to throb. "Are you sure you can handle this?"

"Lila," Turner said. "Go to the window and give Willy a forecast. Tell us what you see, dear."

Lila did as she was told. "I don't believe it," she said. "It's still snowing. It never stopped."

"And what about traffic? Do you see any cars, any pedestrians, any *human activity?*"

"Nothing. They haven't plowed the street since last night."

"You hear that, Willy? Now shall we call an ambulance and have you bleed to death awaiting their arrival, or shall Doctor Turner get down to business?"

"I'm in your hands," Willy said. His face had gone white.

"Very good. Now lie still and try to relax. Lila, love, stroke the boy's brow with a damp cloth from time to time."

Three strips of the torn sheet were soaked through before Turner was able to staunch the bleeding. Lila, meanwhile, had been instructed to sterilize a pair of tweezers and locate a bottle of hydrogen peroxide from the medicine chest. After cleaning the wound, Turner began to delicately pick glass shards from Willy's heel, all the while complaining about the lost reserve fund.

"I trusted you, Willy. What made you go after it, anyway? Were you getting tired of the Old Granddad? Looking for variety? Take note, Lila. More than brand loyalty is at stake here. The boy's a born strayer."

"Why can't you be satisfied it was an accident?" Willy said. "I was reaching for a glass, not the Chivas."

"You expect me to believe that horseshit?"

Willy swiveled his head towards Lila, who was standing beside the table, damp cloth in hand. He was eye level with the red heart appliqué, within inches of her crotch. Now as he spoke he shut his eyes. "Get the bottle of Courvoisier from the bedroom," he said. "Maybe then Turner will see I had no reason to break into the reserve."

Lila fetched the bottle and put it on the table beside the fragments Turner had extracted from Willy's heel.

"Well well," Turner said. His glasses had slid to the tip of his nose while working. "My apologies, Willy. Sorry about the fuss. Lila, dear, pour me a tumbler, would you, please?"

"Maybe that's not such a good idea," she said.

"But of course it is. You want me to have a steady hand when I sew Willy up, don't you?"

12 · *The Trap*

The same day she dropped out of school in order to have more time to paint, Vee took a night job as a cocktail waitress at Peabody's, a bar on Third Avenue with ferns in the window and guacamole on the snack menu. Peabody's was patronized by secretaries and computer analysts, by accountants and confident junior execs. They filled the bar between five and seven and ordered imported beers and white wines from California. They ordered margaritas and brandy Alexanders. Invariably when the crowd had thinned out someone would have left behind a briefcase or an umbrella, a raincoat or a charge card.

Next door to Peabody's was another bar of another sort, a place called the Booby Trap. To get inside the Booby Trap you paid a five-dollar cover charge at the door, which allowed you the privilege, once seated, of ordering drinks from a topless waitress. The Booby Trap didn't serve guacamole or any other kind of food, and had its walls been sandblasted brick like the walls in Peabody's, you probably wouldn't have noticed them. The Booby Trap was dimly lit and withheld more from the eye than it bared.

Both bars were owned and operated by the same man. Sal was in his late thirties and wore his dark hair neatly combed and just over the top of his ears. He'd grown up on Mott Street in Little Italy, above a two-chair barbershop run by his father.

Early one evening Sal summoned Vee to his office. Peabody's and the Booby Trap had separate street entrances, but they were connected by a private cinder-block corridor at the back of the building. Sal's office was off of this corridor.

Vee knocked and entered the office and found Sal seated behind a black metal desk. He wore a checkered sports coat and a knit shirt buttoned at the neck. His hair was in place. "I've got a problem," he said. He told Vee to take a seat and pointed to two closed-circuit television screens mounted on the wall next to his desk. Vee looked at the first screen and immediately recognized the interior of Peabody's. She saw customers she'd just waited on. Only a handful of tables were unoccupied. She then looked at the second screen, at what she guessed was the action on the floor of the Booby Trap. She'd never been inside the bar. The Booby Trap was even more crowded than Peabody's, the tables smaller and closely placed together, the ceiling low. She spotted one topless waitress, then a second, both carrying trays heavy with mixed drinks and bottled beer. But it was the customers who left the strongest impression. Vee saw men in suits, men in work shirts and jeans, men wearing sweaters and turtlenecks. Men of all ages and types, a cross section, as if they'd been randomly snatched from the street.

"One of my girls called in," Sal said. "Told me her uncle died." He lifted his eyebrows, tilted his head. "What are you going to do, these things happen. When my uncle dies I expect I won't come into work either. But still I got a problem. How are things at Peabody's?"

"Fine," Vee said. "It's filling up fast for a Wednesday." She'd been working at Peabody's three months now. She knew when the bar should be full, when empty.

"Look up there," Sal said, pointing to the Booby Trap screen. "It's even busier, isn't it? Here's my problem. I don't like to be shorthanded in either bar, but if I've got a choice I'd rather be short in Peabody's. I make more money in the Trap, and tonight I'm losing money because I'm short a waitress. How much do you make in tips in Peabody's? How much a night?"

Vee was slow to answer. She didn't trust the conversation's sliding direction, its slipperiness.

"Twenty dollars?" Sal asked. "Am I in the ballpark?"

"Sometimes twenty-five," Vee said.

"But more often twenty, and some nights fifteen, and on Mondays and even Tuesdays you're lucky to see that much. Now what if just for tonight I was to guarantee you fifty dollars in tips, whether you make fifty or not? Just for tonight, a one-time thing."

"No," Vee said.

"You haven't even heard what I'm going to say."

Vee crossed her arms. "I'm not working topless, Sal."

"Just relax a minute. Nobody's making you do anything you don't want to do. I'm in a spot is all. I need a favor. I thought you might help me out, just for tonight."

"Why me?"

"You hustle just a little more than the other two girls in Peabody's. I've watched, you're better."

"I've also got a better figure."

"Well that too. I won't deny that. A good figure sells drinks in any bar, that's the kind of world we live in. But you know what the real difference is between the girls in Peabody's and the girls in the Booby Trap? I'm not talking topless here, I'm talking about something that ought to be important to you. The girls in the Trap are making twice the money you're making. Sometimes more. You see Carolyn there?" He pointed to the screen, to a tall brunette with copper skin and a forty-inch bust. Vee felt small just looking at her. "She makes fifty, sixty bucks a night in tips, and that's not counting what I pay her by the hour. I'm just talking tip money. Fifty, sixty bucks, and she's slow, Vee. You stick a fork up her ass she wouldn't move any faster."

Vee started for the door.

"Wait a second," Sal said. "Wait." He held up both hands as

if being robbed at gunpoint. "Excuse me. I didn't mean what I just said. I'm not thinking tonight. I'm short a girl and I'm losing money and I'm not thinking. I apologize."

"I still don't want to do this, Sal."

"You don't *have* to. You don't have to do anything you don't want to do. I just needed a favor and I thought you might help. So I made a mistake. I've been wrong before. What is it, your husband you're worried about?"

Here he goes again, Vee thought. As a matter of fact, Ron hadn't even crossed her mind. Right now he'd be finishing his supper and getting ready to leave the apartment for one of the night classes he taught at the university. What would his reaction be if he learned she was working topless? Another man might get rough, make rude accusations. Another man might smolder, feel humiliated. What would Ron feel? He never asked her about Peabody's, never asked about the people she worked with, about the customers.

"What is it?" Sal was saying. "I'm just trying to figure this thing out. If it's not your husband, what? You think I'll be taking advantage? Is that it? By working topless you'll be exploited or oppressed or whatever they call it? Am I close? Let me ask you a simple question, Vee. What do the waitresses wear in Peabody's? They wear what you're wearing right now, am I right? A short skirt and a Peabody's T-shirt. That's the uniform. Not exactly clothes you wear to Sunday mass. And what about the girls in the Trap? They wear a short skirt too, but instead of a T-shirt they go naked from the waist up. I'm telling you there's less difference here than meets the eye. The real difference is something you can't see, and that's the amount of money being made. You ever get touched when you're working Peabody's?"

"What do you mean?" Vee said.

"Touched. You ever get touched. Say some guy in a suit, one of these business types that always comes in, thinks the world of himself, doesn't know shit from shoe leather, excuse me, does this sort of guy ever put his hand on your shoulder while ordering a drink? Maybe a couple of his pals from the office are with him, he's trying to be smooth. You know what I'm saying? Or maybe the same guy, he's had a couple drinks now, a couple slams, he's beginning to get sloppy, maybe his tie's crooked, maybe he's got a little guacamole on his sleeve, he ever put his arm around your waist as he orders another round? That kind of thing ever happen?"

"It's annoying as hell," Vee said.

"I happen to agree. That's why we've got a policy in the Trap. You're going to appreciate this. Wait right here." Sal disappeared from the office, and seconds later Vee saw him fill the Booby Trap screen on the wall. Sal picked up a cocktail napkin from an empty table and waved it and smiled blandly at the camera. Twenty seconds later he was back in his office.

"You see this?" he said. "You see what's printed on this napkin? 'The Booby Trap. No Touching Permitted.' Every napkin says the same thing, and every drink comes with one of these napkins. If a guy orders five drinks he gets five napkins, just so he doesn't forget. And if he touches one of my girls, if he even touches her elbow, even by accident, he gets the boot. You see Larry over there?" Sal pointed to a corner of the screen, to a doorway blocked by a large immobile black man wearing a spaghetti-strap T-shirt. "Larry wrestled in high school, right here in New York. He's a city kid like me. Larry's trouble, and anyone with eyes in his head knows it. A good bouncer keeps a business strong."

Vee thought Larry might make a good subject for her to paint. Standing so still, so tall and wide, like a column of poured concrete, he'd model for hours without question or complaint, his eyes fixed on some distant spot.

"I'll tell you who's being exploited," Sal went on. "It's those guys out there." He waved his hand at the screen. "They shell out five bucks before they're even inside the door. For what? To see a pair of tits they even breathe on they get thrown into the street. Where are the real boobs in this picture? I'll tell you. They're sitting at the tables, ordering drinks that are watered-down and overpriced. And when half these guys leave they overtip because they're embarrassed, they feel funny, maybe they've been doing something they shouldn't have been doing. They've got wives at home, they've got girlfriends, but they come here because they've got a need. Who knows what it is. Every guy's got a different reason, I don't even want to think about it. It's not the girls working topless who are being exploited, it's the customers, these guys here. Why do you think this place is called the Booby Trap? I'm amazed every time I think about it. A guy drops twenty, thirty bucks to get drunk and see tits in a dark room. Who's being taken? The girls going topless are making money."

"You're making money," Vee said. "You're making more than they are, and you're not walking around half-dressed."

"If I wasn't making money, the girls wouldn't be making money. Who pays the bills around here, anyway? Who got the liquor license and the loan from the bank? Not Carolyn out there. This is my business. Why shouldn't I be making money? I *like* making money. Making money makes me happy."

Vee thought of Ron teaching his night class at the university. He was making money too. Did teaching make him happy? She could see him standing at the lectern, see him glancing at his notes on a yellow pad of legal paper. He'd have unstrapped his watch from his wrist and placed it next to the notes. Vee could see him standing there, concentrated, taking questions, all of his weight first on one leg, then the other. She could hear the sound of his voice, imagine the lecture. But could Ron imagine her at work? He'd never been to Peabody's. He'd never even asked her how much she earned. She could work topless and he'd never know. Never mind what his feelings might be, he'd never know. Feelings wouldn't be his to have. But why would she want to work topless? Fifty dollars couldn't buy much of anything. Vee looked at the Booby Trap screen. All those men out there, drinking drinks and thinking thoughts, sitting almost meekly at the tables, not being able to touch except with their eyes. Sal had said it was the men who were being taken, and that was true, Vee could see that. But what about the waitresses? They were being used as bait to lure the customer from his money. They got paid for this service, a service they performed for Sal, mostly with tips that came from the customer. A waitress performed a service for Sal and the customer paid the bill. Sal had a good thing going.

Vee said, "How much do you think you're losing tonight by being shorthanded?"

"A couple hundred dollars," Sal said. "Call it two hundred. Why?"

"You said you needed a favor."

Sal glanced at Vee's chest. "You going to help me out?"

"I could," Vee said. "What if we split the two hundred you stand to make with my help?"

"I can't do that, Vee. I don't operate that way."

"You can't make the two hundred without me."

"I said I don't work like that."

"Then make an exception. That's what I'm doing, that's what you're asking me to do. I work topless and hustle drinks, and we split the two hundred. Whatever tips I make I keep."

"You want a hundred *plus* tips?"

"That's right. Plus my hourly wage. And tomorrow night I'm back in Peabody's."

"I don't believe this."

Vee started for the door.

"Wait a second," Sal said. "Hold on. You think you're pretty smart, don't you? All right, we do it your way, but first I got to see what you look like." He passed his hand across his mouth.

"First I've got to be sure we have a deal," Vee said.

"All right, we got a deal. For one night only."

"For one night only," Vee said. She pulled her Peabody's T-shirt over her head.

13 · *The Target*

Stale from a day of driving, Willy pulled off the highway about forty miles south of Casper, Wyoming, and onto a gravel lot in front of a roadhouse tavern. A six-passenger pickup was the only other vehicle in the lot.

Inside, he ordered a bottle of beer and bought a pack of cigarettes from a vending machine. The tavern looked like others he'd seen in the last five months as he slowly made his way across the continent. He'd driven from one city to another, not hurrying, eating and sleeping and sometimes finding work in places he'd only known as names on maps.

Three days after Willy had graduated from college his father died of a heart attack. He stayed with his mother through the summer and ran errands, filed claims with Blue Cross, sat around. He cooked the evening supper and tended to the lawn, but mainly he wondered where he'd go when the time came to leave.

Just once during that long sad summer did Willy's mother mention the vacation traveling she and her husband had enjoyed over the years. She and Willy were sitting in aluminum lawn chairs on the patio in the backyard. The evening was cool for mid-August, and Willy's mother wore a sweater draped over her shoulders and sipped from a thimble of Drambuie.

"Your father and I liked to get away and be by ourselves for a few weeks every summer," she said. "I know that might sound selfish, but it wasn't. You and your brother needed to be away from us too. When both of you were still small, I don't think you'd even started school at the time, your father and I drove up to Nova Scotia. Do you remember when we left you and Matt with my mother?"

Willy nodded, but he didn't remember.

"We had a flat tire and a burst radiator hose before we even reached the Canadian border, but we couldn't have cared less. Nothing bothered us on that trip. Later on we went to the Bahamas, to Mexico and Venezuela, Europe. Lots of different places. It seemed the older you and Matt got, the farther afield we allowed ourselves to travel."

"Didn't you make a trip to Haiti in there somewhere?"

"Yes we did. We did Haiti all right. I loved Haiti and your father hated it. He got sick and was miserable the entire time we were down there. Eight days and seven nights of bad temper and running to the bathroom, and all on account of something he ate the first hour we were in Port-au-Prince. . . .

"But you know what's odd, Willy? I keep thinking about this, I don't know why. In all those summers of traveling, of carefully planned getaways, neither your father or I was ever west of Pennsylvania. We never really saw the country we lived in. Doesn't that strike you as odd, as some sort of miscalculation? What made us think Bermuda or Ireland or wherever we went was any better than a place like Kentucky? I'm not saying they aren't better, I don't know, I can't compare. We thought to really travel you had to *leave*. If you didn't need a passport, where were you going? When I was a little girl I always wanted to go to Kentucky. You know why?"

"The Colonel," Willy said, trying to joke. "Fried chicken."

"Almost as silly. My mother used to tell me the grass in Kentucky was as blue as the ocean."

Willy left home in September, his belongings piled in the backseat and trunk of his car. In Cincinnati he spent three weeks working at a car wash, scouring rubber floor mats and whitewall tires with a steam gun as long as a rifle. In Rapid City, South Dakota, he worked nearly a month as a day laborer on a construction site for subsidized housing, a government contract, the pace almost leisurely.

Now he was in Wyoming where the wind numbed your face and the first snow had long since fallen. He was heading southwest, Denver his next target. He figured to be there by midnight, stay a few weeks, and then push west and on to California, a land his parents had only seen on movie and television screens.

Willy ran a hand across his face and tried to unwind. His pants bagged out at the knees from too many hours behind the wheel. He drank from his beer and looked at the lit up Coors display reflected in the long mirror behind the bar. Then he saw the pool table in the middle of the tavern floor, a dart board hanging on the back wall, a jukebox tucked into the corner by a bathroom door marked "Gents." Taped to the cash register behind the bar was a magazine photo of a bare-bottomed playmate holding a sign that read "Liquor in the Front, Poker in the Rear."

Raucous laughter from a corner table drew Willy's attention. Five men crowded a Formica table and shared a pitcher of beer. Empty pitchers, Willy couldn't see exactly how many, sat on the floor by their feet. The men wore green coveralls that identified them with some company or agency, maybe a highway department, maybe a sanitation crew. One of the men wore a gold baseball cap that concealed his eyes.

Feeling more like himself with a beer in his hand, Willy pointed to the dart board with his bottle and spoke to the men in an easy voice.

"Anybody want to throw some darts?"

No reply. Willy shrugged and wandered over to the dart board alone. The board was a pie with equal pieces, the whole subdivided into twenty numbered sections that radiated from the center. Six darts with brass points and plastic tail ends stuck in a cluster to the board. Willy collected the darts and stepped back about ten feet.

The first four darts, tossed in quick succession, landed in a pattern that conformed roughly to the cardinal points on a compass. The men stole looks at one another, shifted their feet. Willy tossed the fifth dart, a high-arcing lob that landed a fraction of an inch from the center of the board. He'd always been good at darts, at throwing and finding the target. He addressed the men, obviously pleased with his performance, and held up the sixth dart.

He said, "A buck says one of you boys can't hit the bull's-eye." He smiled a friendly smile, relieved to be in company after the loneliness of the highway.

The men looked at one another with glassy eyes. They drank their beer. The man with the gold baseball cap—his friends called him Jimbo—finally swiveled in his seat and waved Willy over. Willy walked to the table, dart between fingers like a cigarette.

"I can hit the bull's-eye just about any time I feel like it," Jimbo said, taking the dart from Willy.

Willy waited for Jimbo to get up and toss the dart. Jimbo didn't get up. He didn't stir. His friends looked on.

"I said I can *hit* the bull's-eye just about any time I *feel* like it." Jimbo stepped on certain words, making his point felt as well as heard. "Thing is, right now I *don't* feel like it, so get the fuck lost."

Laughter and foot stomping from Jimbo's friends.

Willy sucked in his breath as he walked back to the bar, realizing he'd overstepped himself. The men were strangers after all. *He* was a stranger. He considered leaving, getting away in his car, when Jimbo began speaking to his friends in a voice intended to be overheard. Willy sensed entrapment but wouldn't break away. He ordered another bottle of beer and listened to Jimbo.

"Know that pup Preston got from the shelter?"

Jimbo's friends nodded, sipped their beer.

"Frisky thing," Jimbo said, "but dumb as a door, no sense at all. Last week the dog's playing in the big ravine behind Preston's place, the one with the coyote burrows, just sniffing and barking and raising a ruckus. Preston was in his house when he heard the commotion but paid it no mind. Dog would bark at anything, Preston says. Bark at a leaky faucet.

"So what happened, one coyote came out of his burrow and began this long howl. Preston said the hair on his neck stood straight up at the sound of it. Well he tore ass over elbow out of the house, and by the time he got to the ravine the dog was surrounded by a *pack* of coyotes, maybe fifteen of them all told. Old Preston dropped his jaw—and you know him, he doesn't scare easy.

"By this time the dog was slinking on his belly in the middle of this howling circle, just shivering and not making a sound no more, tail curled back up between his legs. Preston shouted and swore and started heaving rocks, big chunks of stone, but it didn't do no good. He said it was like the coyotes were waiting for a signal from one of their own, and when just the right moment came they all at once pounced and ripped the living shit out of the dog. Ten seconds was all it took to disembowel the pup.

"That's what happens," Jimbo said. "Dog ought to know he can't go messing with no pack of coyotes."

Willy stared at Jimbo and imagined himself saying, *Ten bucks says the asshole with the gold hat can't even hit the fucking wall.* But he didn't say that. He didn't say a word. He slid off his stool and threw a pair of dollar bills on the bar and removed himself from the tavern, counting his steps as he went.

14 · *Models and Idols*

Willy wondered whether to trust his eyes. He was standing at the corner of Clay and Kearny, waiting for the light to change, the afternoon *Examiner* tucked under his arm. On the other side of the street, also waiting for the light, was a woman who looked familiar. Too familiar not to notice. She stared openly at Willy, stared as he stared at her.

Vee? he thought.

The light changed. People moved through the intersection quickly and with purpose.

"Willy?" she said.

The two of them stopped in the middle of the street, in front of a city bus with a grinning driver, and embraced awkwardly. They'd been high school friends, even dated a couple of times one summer, but how long had it been since they'd seen each other? Six years?

"What are you doing in San Francisco?" Willy said.

"I *live* here."

"But I thought you were married and lived in New York."

"Divorced five months ago," Vee said brightly. She held up a ringless hand like a certificate of good health.

Willy took Vee by the elbow and guided her to the other side of the street, the side she'd just come from.

"Listen," he said, "you think you'd like to get a drink? Catch up?"

Vee frowned, looked past Willy's shoulder.

"What's the matter?"

"I'm on my way to work," she said.

"At five in the afternoon?"

"I'm waitressing. During the day I go to school."

Willy nodded. He'd heard, though he couldn't remember from whom, that in New York Vee had worked odd jobs at night and painted in a rented studio during the day. He had no idea what sort of painting she did, or why she was now back in school.

"But I could always call in sick," she said, her fingers passing, just a feather's touch, across Willy's arm. "The job's not that important."

Willy took a handful of change from his pocket. "Call," he said. "Call before I ask somebody else."

Vee lifted her chin and laughed. "All right, but only if you promise to buy me some wine. *Good* wine, Willy. Not that crap we used to drink in high school."

Willy led Vee to a bar down by the Embarcadero. They took a table at the back of the barroom and ordered a bottle.

"You have to tell me all about yourself," Vee said. She had her elbows propped up on the table and held her hands together. Her straight blond hair was cut at the shoulder, her skin clear. She'd always been a pretty girl, but the last time Willy had seen her they'd both been teenagers. She looked as fine as his memory of her, though she looked different too. Her breasts were fuller, her face lean, her hands strong and big, almost out of scale with the rest of her body.

"I moved out here about a year and a half ago," Willy began, his eyes wandering over the freshness of Vee. She was close enough to touch. If he leaned across the table he'd be able to run his tongue along her neck. He offered her a cigarette, but she declined by shaking her head, smiling, pushing a hand through her hair.

"What do you do?" she said.

"I work for a steamship agency. Office job on California Street. A couple of days a week I'm down on the pier."

"Doing what?"

"Taking care of documentation, making sure our cargo clears through customs without any trouble. It's just ordinary stuff. Beans and coffee, tape decks from Japan, sneakers from Yugoslavia. But right now I want to hear about you and your divorce. Your husband turned out to be a stinker, huh?"

"A real shit, Willy. I had no idea."

"You want to tell me about it?"

Vee had married when she was an undergraduate, in the middle of her sophomore year. Her parents were disappointed, they said she was too young, they told her to be patient, but what could they really do? Vee was in love and wouldn't be denied. Anyway, most of her tuition was paid for by a merit scholarship. Her parents had no leverage. The guy she married taught art history. Ron eventually became a full professor, but back when he first met Vee he was an assistant and still worried about tenure. He was jumpy about tenure for a couple of years.

One of the courses Ron taught was a survey of twentieth-century architecture. Vee enrolled because she had no choice, the course was required of art majors, but modern buildings bored her and she ended up drawing sketches of Ron as he lectured. She had drawn sketches of people and things since she was five years old. Ron heard about the sketches from someone and invited Vee to an exhibition of seventeenth-century Dutch drawings at the Metropolitan. The next day they went to the Frick to look at the Whistlers, and the day after that Ron helped Vee pick out some rice paper at an artist's supply house on Canal Street.

Ron was tall and rangy and seemed unhappy, almost forlorn, whenever he left Vee after one of their excursions. He wore a beard and Levi cords and an old Harris tweed sports coat. Vee began to fall for Ron and made no effort to catch herself. They were married during the winter break, two months after they started dating, and flew to Jamaica for their honeymoon. Vee was nineteen and Ron thirty.

Vee wanted to be a painter, and though you couldn't have called her ambitious, at least not at first if only because her ideas about painting were unformed, she worked hard and had a calculating mind. Other kids in the art department were sewing themselves in rolls of canvas and lying on gallery floors, or typing proposals for massive art projects and presenting the proposals, framed and wired to hang, as finished pieces. Performances were staged almost daily. One student walked across campus wearing nothing but a wristwatch. When he was arrested he surrendered his watch to the police and his piece stopped. The students in the department who elected to study painting talked theory and kept their eyes on the Minimalists in SoHo. Vee studied draftsmanship and human anatomy and drew figures from live models. The models were supplied by the school and their fee was included in Vee's tuition. Half the time she had the painting studios to herself. No one really noticed her.

"I can't imagine you going unnoticed," Willy said.

Vee leaned forward. "What do you mean?"

"I mean," Willy said. How should he say this? "I mean you seem to know what you want. Even as a kid you were like that. You're determined, Vee, it's almost a physical characteristic, like hair color or the shape of a nose. People can spot these traits in other people."

"What else do you see?" Vee said.

Willy pondered for effect. "I see a divorced woman. No, I see a *single* woman who wants to get on with her life. She's determined to be happy, to do what *she* wants to do. And look at this, I see something else. There's a man in her future. He's very close at hand."

"Naturally," Vee said, but suddenly she was sad. "Until we

just met on the street, I hadn't thought about Ron in weeks. Do you know what a pain that can be, trying to forget somebody you hate?"

Willy glanced at Vee's wineglass. His own was empty. Should he pour himself another, or wait until she finished? "You like the wine?" he said.

Vee sat back and took a sip, pursing her lips as she swallowed. "Just talking about all this makes me feel odd. Maybe we should get something to eat, Willy, talk about other things."

"Absolutely not," Willy said. "Tell me more. I want to hate this ex-husband of yours just as much as you do."

She'd drawn hundreds of sketches of Ron—Ron teaching, Ron sleeping, Ron eating lo mein out of a paper container over the sink—before she put his figure on canvas. Before she put his *portrait* on canvas. No one at school was painting portraits. One of Vee's teachers, a painter himself, was of the opinion painting had died and gone to museum heaven. Painting's in the graveyard, he said. It's already disappeared, we just haven't noticed. He advised Vee to make films, to switch majors, to do anything but paint, especially portraits. Portraiture, he said, had become the province of photography. Vee argued that she wasn't a camera. Her teacher told her she'd be wasting her time. Don't embarrass yourself, he said.

But Vee thought differently. If no one was making a serious effort to paint portraits, where was the competition? The field was open and waiting to be made new again.

Things happened very quickly after that. Near the end of her sophomore year she exhibited a group of portraits at the school's gallery and a critic from the *Village Voice* saw the show and wrote a short review. That he later tried to date Vee, not realizing she was already married, was of no consequence. The review had been written, the word passed. Ron predicted big things and didn't interfere when, in the middle of her junior year, Vee dropped out of school to devote all of her time to painting. A downtown gallery had approached her and promised two shows in the coming year. She was now twenty years old.

Her portraits resisted easy description. For lack of a better word you might have called her painted figures expressionistic, while her backgrounds, what she used to fill her pictures in with, were almost entirely abstract. She worked with a lot of paint because she liked the added texture, though she avoided bright colors, preferring the muted somber tones of faded old masters she'd seen in art books. Her style was a conscious gathering of preceding styles, some of them very old, blended in a combination that was unexpected but did not confound or mystify. People were grateful. There was already enough obfuscation in contemporary art. Vee painted from live models—she'd tried painting from photographs, she'd tried painting from memory, the results were unexceptional—and strove for an emotional likeness of her subject. The portraits of Ron were typically sullen and depressed and very compact, though once she left school she began using a wider brush and her range literally broadened.

About this time Vee and Ron grew apart. She had pretty much stopped using him as a model, but whether this was the cause of their deteriorating relationship or just a symptom was hard to tell. She rented a studio three blocks from their apartment and painted during the day. In the evening she worked as a cocktail waitress.

But she was having other problems too, and not just with Ron. Her attitude towards painting was shifting picture by picture, taking her in a direction she found difficult to grasp. Her figures got more primitive, more generic Ron said, and less like individuals. More and more the *personality* of her subject, of her model, was left unfocused. Vee understood the point of portraiture was to capture a particular person in a particular time. She understood she was failing to do this, that her latest paintings were hardly portraits at all. She started to worry.

But she kept painting, she didn't know what else to do. When she began to obliterate key features, especially in the face, her gallery told her she was crazy. A good pair of eyes, just the eyes, could sell a picture. She didn't listen. Soon afterwards she eliminated clothing or any trapping that might identify a subject with a specific time or place. In the foreground of one of her paintings you'd see a lone nude figure, without eyes or hair, without ears. There would be a nose, a mouth, and just a hint of the figure's gender. In the background you'd see an abstract wash of muted color and muddy texture and nothing more. Vee felt with each succeeding painting she was working closer to the center of whatever it was that kept nagging her. For once she didn't question her motives. She didn't calculate. Every afternoon she took a short nap after she'd finished painting for the day, and while she napped—twice this happened—an image came to her. Not a dream, an image. She'd see a pair of hands, strong and shaped well, perhaps male, perhaps female, washing a window with a paper towel and a bottle of blue Windex.

Vee's last show at the gallery, nearly two years after she quit school, got a very bad press. No one knew what she was doing. Ron didn't even go to the opening. He'd seen the paintings in the studio and hardly said a word. Only one painting sold, one of twelve, and that to an anonymous buyer who turned out to be Vee's father. Of all people, her father. One of her friends had called him and said the show was in trouble. This was very depressing to Vee, but only in the most obvious ways. Tuned in to her own private channel, working the dial, she was convinced she would eventually see what was hiding from her. People said she was painting badly, and maybe she was, but that didn't stop her.

Vee had to use the bathroom.

When she returned Willy said, "There's something I don't follow. Why did people think you were painting badly?"

"I'd lost some confidence. You could see it when you looked at the paintings."

Willy frowned. "You decide to paint portraits, right? You

have this early success, and then not long afterwards your work begins to change, which only seems smart. Don't repeat yourself and all that. So the portraits become something other than portraits. Instead of painting an identifiable person, you're painting someone you've made up, someone you've created."

"Which turned out to be harder. Harder in my case, anyway."

"Okay, harder in your case. But wouldn't the skill you brought to portraiture, the technique, be brought to the new work as well? You already had the skill."

"The skill isn't the painting. Technique is just a way to get the painting painted. With the new work I had to dig down into myself for the raw material. I think I mentioned this didn't happen all at once. I mean I didn't suddenly give up portraiture. The work evolved from one thing to the other. Maybe it evolved pretty fast, but then I was painting fast, that's the only important thing I was doing. And once I started really digging I began coming up with these strange figures."

"People without faces," Willy said.

"People *with* faces, but lacking certain features."

"Were you still painting from live models?"

"I was still using models, but only as a visual aid, mainly for perspective. The models weren't the figures I painted, I was pulling the figures out of myself, and each canvas got more peculiar than the one before it. And yet I couldn't stop. The figures presented this problem that had to be solved."

"You mean some kind of formal problem?"

"No, the kind of problem psychologists like. An emotional problem. A *personal* problem. When you're lost you try and find a way out. And I finally did, I found a way out, Willy, only it wasn't what I'd expected."

One Saturday while browsing in a bookstore on lower Broadway, Vee came across a catalogue of Cycladic art and culture, and as she picked up the heavy book and studied its cover she had an odd sensation. *The catalogue was looking back at her.* She flipped through its pages and color plates, heard its spine crack. Vee was only dimly aware a Cycladic civilization had even existed, yet the figures she'd lately been painting resembled—in some cases almost looked like copies—of the photographed objects in the catalogue. She sat down on a short aluminum stepladder in a corner of the bookstore and skimmed the introduction. She learned the Cycladic Islands were clustered southeast of mainland Greece and north of Crete in the Aegean Sea. Around 3000 B.C. artisans began hoarding blocks of marble that washed ashore and then used them to carve small anthropomorphic figures—idols, the book said—which they later buried with their dead.

Vee read no further. She took her wallet from her knapsack and counted her money, but after paying the sales tax the catalogue would cost more than twenty-five dollars, and she only had eleven dollars, maybe twelve counting the change in her pocket. Not enough, she thought, but that's okay. Thinking, plotting, her eyes panning the store like a concealed camera, she wandered over to a table piled high with remaindered novels and knocked a stack to the floor with a nudge from her elbow. While stooping over to pick them up she eased the catalogue into her knapsack.

What excited Vee about the Cycladic idols was that they were nearly featureless. She sat at a worktable in her studio and pored over the photographs in the catalogue. The text indicated the idols might at one time have been painted, though they'd been underground for such a long time that now you saw nothing more than naked marble encrusted with dirt and age and random deposits of calcium carbonate. The idols did not have eyes or ears. They did not have mouths or hair or cheekbones, yet human characteristics were discernible. Noses, for instance, and arms folded across the chest. An incised triangle might represent the pubic patch, a graceful moon-shaped cleft divide the buttocks.

The connection between these objects and Vee's own painted

figures wouldn't let her go, but all the same something didn't feel right. The idols in the catalogue were more expressive than her figures. They were cleaner and more sharply focused, as if they vibrated at a greater frequency. Her own figures, so similar at first, were slow, almost sluggish in comparison. She thought, What was it that compelled the Cycladic people to carve these objects? She wasn't sure. And then another thought piggybacked onto the first. What was it that compelled her to paint? Did she have any business being a painter? She thought about this. She looked out her window. And then a simple aching reason for it all, a reason as likely as any other, leapt out at her. She painted because she wanted to be famous. She wanted to be famous because she wanted her parents' attention. They'd pulled back around the time her baby brother died. Patrick had gotten sick and expired in virtually the same moment, and only a few days later he was forever underground and nothing was quite the same again. There it is, Vee thought, a true confession, woefully banal but true. She couldn't have been calmer just then had she washed down ten milligrams of Valium with a glass of warm milk. She didn't have to paint. Nor did she have to resent her parents until she was famous enough for them to take real notice of her. She could do what she wanted. Her parents would take care of themselves. They always had.

But she didn't stop painting, not then, not right away, though she did cut her schedule back and used the free time to sketch and read, to putter. Painting was something she rushed through in the morning. By one in the afternoon her brushes would be rinsed and already dry.

She'd been gazing into her glass, speaking in a tone that carried no further than the small table, when Willy interrupted.

"My turn," he said. "Help yourself to the wine."

Coming back from the bathroom he noticed Vee's glass, as well as his own, had been refilled. The wine bottle was now nearly empty. Should he order another? Yes. First things first.

"I have a question," he said, once again seated across from Vee. "Your parents. I don't remember them very well, yet it wasn't all that long ago that we were growing up. Mickey Dekker's mother and father I can recall as if I'd seen them yesterday, but I'm not sure I'd recognize your parents even if you pointed them out to me. They kept to themselves."

"They've always been private," Vee said. "Always devoted to one another."

"But not so devoted to their daughter?"

Vee shrugged. "I was by myself a lot. The only time the three of us ate together was on the weekends, and even then they often went out. I'm not bothered so much anymore, though when I was little I sometimes felt—I was going to say *abandoned*, but that's not right. Even *neglected* would be too strong. I was provided for, just like everybody else we knew. I had birthday parties, new clothes, things we took for granted, we expected, as if children had always lived like that. My mother made sure I was a reader, my father encouraged me to draw. They just weren't *around* so much, they didn't make themselves available. We'd be under the same roof, but in separate rooms. The house was always quiet, that's what I remember. If my brother had lived we would have been a different family. There would have been more activity, more noise. I often think about Patrick, especially what he'd look like. Once you can picture a person, even if the picture is wrong, you're free to imagine other things about them."

Willy had another question for Vee and didn't hesitate to ask. An hour of talk and a bottle of wine and they were again becoming friends. "Just curious," he said, "but why did you marry Ron?"

"Ron needed me. At least he needed someone *like* me. That was such a good feeling in the beginning, so new, the first year or two."

"Being needed?"

"Yes, being needed every minute. My parents loved from a distance. That was their specialty, that's what I was used to. They weren't any good at close range, at seeing what was in front of them. A certain remove was required." She was staring. "Do you understand?"

Willy nodded.

Her favorite model, favorite because the girl never asked for money, was an art student from the university. She was at the studio one morning and Vee was "preparing" her before starting work on canvas. The girl stood in the middle of the floor, naked, arms crossed, goose bumps on her flesh because the studio had a cement floor and was chilly. Vee mixed dirt and ground chalk with water in a galvanized bucket and applied it to the model's body. The effect she was trying to achieve was that of an ancient weathered layer, as if the model had just been pulled from the ground.

Vee was on her knees, using her hand as both scoop and brush to spread a thin layer of the dirt and chalk mix across the model's legs, across her thighs and cold buttocks, when Ron chose to pay a visit to the studio. He opened the door without knocking and took a step inside and then froze, his hand stuck to the doorknob. Vee looked over and said hello and kept working. "What's up?" she said. She disliked being interrupted. Ron stared as Vee brushed the mix onto the model's hip with the edge of her hand. Her movements were deft and knowing. She looked as if she'd done this a thousand times.

"What the hell are you doing?" Ron said.

"Working." His tone irritated her. Everything about him was beginning to irritate her.

Ron continued to stare, his hand still gripping the doorknob. "I thought the idea was to put paint on canvas."

Vee didn't look up. "I'm just about to."

"I don't know *what* you're about to do," he said, "but I'll tell you something. You've never touched me like that."

Vee looked over at Ron with a start, but he was already out the door and banging down the stairs. What was the problem? she thought. The model was just a model, a mannequin with breath. It wasn't as if she'd been caught in bed with her legs wrapped around the girl's neck.

Late that afternoon Vee went to her job as a cocktail waitress at Peabody's. When she finally got home a little after midnight Ron was still up, sitting at the kitchen table and drinking from a fifth of Seagram's Seven. There was no glass on the table. No ice, no mixer. The bottle was half-empty, at least until Ron took a long sloppy swig, and then it was a good deal less than half-empty. Vee wondered where the whiskey had come from. They never kept hard liquor in the apartment. She liked a glass of brandy to unwind after coming home from work and always kept a bottle in the cabinet near the sink, but this was for her, not Ron. Ron only drank when drinking was expected of him— one of the dean's dinner parties, New Year's Eve, a wedding or a wake. Alcohol did not make him happy. More than one drink and he was liable to get belligerent. Friends and colleagues wound up insulted. One drink was his limit. One drink and he was fine. Two drinks and Ron was not Ron, he was the guy you told other people to avoid.

Vee gave a wide berth to the kitchen table and pressed her knapsack to her chest. Never had she known Ron to drink the better half of a fifth of whiskey. She thought of leaving.

"*Cunt,*" he shouted. Vee winced and he said it again, and then again. It was as if he were hitting her over the head with the nearest blunt object, anything at all, a heavy ashtray, the heel of a shoe.

"Ron, please. . . ."

He rose from the table and made a drunken lunge for her. Vee jumped back until she came up against the refrigerator. The coolness of the door startled her. This kitchen is too small, she thought, the whole apartment is too small. Ron lunged again, his eyes bright but heavy-lidded, showing nothing but glassy black pupils, and grabbed Vee's shoulder. This time he managed to stay on his feet.

"Stop it!" she screamed.

He was standing tall now, a full head above Vee, when he

cocked his arm and aimed his fist for her face and took his shot. But he missed, and no one could have been more surprised than Ron, you could see the surprise as his eyes went wide and showed too much white. He missed, he was double-vision drunk, and his fist slammed into the refrigerator door with a dull metal thud that knocked over bottles and containers inside. He gave out a cry of pain and looked at his crumpled hand, long enough for Vee to shake herself loose and dash for the door.

She spent the night with a girlfriend who had a loft on Broome Street. The next day she moved into her studio and had the locks changed and a metal gate put on the window. She never went back to the apartment again. Ever. A guy she knew, a weight lifter who used to model at the school when she was still a student, packed up her belongings at the apartment and brought them to the studio. Before the week was out Vee had filed for divorce.

Willy poured more wine into Vee's glass and then sat back, hands laced behind his head. "Did Ron ever apologize?"

"No," she said. She regarded her ringless hand. "Now I'm in a new city. . . ."

"And you're back in school," Willy said, but he was still thinking about the meanness that had spilled from Ron. "Why do you think he got so violent? Did he really believe you were fooling around with that model?"

"This sounds terrible," Vee said, "but I'm not sure Ron ever loved me at all. What he loved was being loved. That's the *need* I was telling you about before. He loved that I was in love with him." She stopped and picked up her wineglass, then put it down again. "I don't know what sort of teacher he'll become, but as a husband he was awful. Teachers are supposed to teach, they're supposed to give instruction. It's hard to imagine Ron giving anybody anything. When he finally figured out I'd stopped loving him he got angry."

"Well I'm glad you're away from him," Willy said with some heat. "What's happening with your painting, anyway? I didn't know you were such a celebrity."

"I was hardly a celebrity, Willy. Right now going to school and working nights are about all I can manage."

"What are you studying?"

"Art history."

"Ron's field."

"Except I'm not going to teach. I don't know what I'll do. Maybe museum work. About a month ago I got a letter from a girlfriend back in New York. You know what she said? Ron's dating another one of his students. Probably someone who adores him."

"That figures." Willy shook his head with exaggerated disgust. "That figures, doesn't it." Then he lowered his voice and leaned forward. "Maybe I could have Ron shot. What do you think? Sounds reasonable, doesn't it? I know some people on the waterfront, Vee. Very serious about their work. They do things right."

Vee laughed out loud and reached for Willy's hands. "It's fun to be with you, Willy. You cheer me up."

Willy smiled his best smile. "That's just the wine talking," he said.

15 · *High Noon*

Vee poured the wine over her head and let it run down her face
and neck and over her breasts. She poured the wine again and
it ran down her belly and over her hips and thighs and between
her legs where drops of it collected in her patch of dark blond
hair. Willy dropped to his knees and pressed his face to the wet
patch and ran his tongue between the soft folds of flesh and
tasted the dark red wine and tasted Vee. She poured the bottle
again and the wine splashed across his face pressed into her and
the wine ran down her legs and he felt the muscles in her
thighs flutter and her legs buckle and he let her fall, but gently,
with an arm across the small of her back so she wouldn't hurt
herself when she landed in the grass.

Willy drank from the bottle and felt light-headed and happy.
Vee was now lying in the grass with the noonday sun shining
on her face and blond hair and the sun on her breasts and the
leanness of her belly. She was smiling with her mouth open
and eyes closed when Willy climbed between her legs and lay
down on top of her and began to gently stroke the inside of her.
The sun was on the back of his neck and shoulders and burning
his backside and the soles of his feet. He kissed Vee's eyelids
and kissed her open mouth and stroked gently between her legs
and tried to make the moment last, and it lasted.

Afterwards he dressed himself with calmness. He stepped into his blue cotton shorts and slipped on his T-shirt and sandals and put his sunglasses back on his face. Vee lay in the grass and watched Willy dress, and when he finished dressing she dressed and he watched her.

16 · *The List*

Zinnias or lilacs? Vee thought. What type of flower do you buy your lover after you've been living with him for precisely five weeks? She'd already dismissed the roses as too predictable, the white peonies because the petals had begun to droop.

Willy was working down at the pier. He'd gotten a phone call at seven A.M., while they were still in bed. Two tons of tea from Mangalore had been misplaced. "Mis*placed?*" he said into the phone. "How can two tons of anything get misplaced?" He ran a hand across his face. Today was Saturday, his day off, which only made the call more aggravating.

Vee ended up buying zinnias *and* lilacs. She'd already been to the butcher, the greengrocer and the liquor store. She hoped she hadn't spent too much. When she moved in with Willy they agreed she should quit waitressing and accelerate her schedule at graduate school. The sooner she completed her studies and found a job, the sooner she'd be happy and better able to contribute her share.

As Vee headed back to the apartment with bags in both hands, she felt the weight of the load in her neck and shoulders. The orange plastic sack with the liquor was the heaviest. Willy had requested a bottle of Jack Daniels and a dry white wine before he'd left in the morning. Vee had wanted a Beaujolais for herself, which meant three bottles to cart home. Nearly everything she was carrying would be consumed by the end of the weekend. Veal tonight, Caesar salad on Sunday. Willy would race through the whiskey and wine as if a penalty awaited him for drinking too slowly. Even the flowers might not make it to Monday.

She stopped at the corner, next to a mailbox, and shifted her bags as she waited for the light to change. During the morning she'd begun a letter to her parents. After Willy had gulped coffee and driven off to work, Vee sat at the kitchen table, a pen and pad of paper before her. She had started the letter by announcing she was living with somebody they might remember, somebody who made her feel good, as good as she'd felt in a long time. All of which took three sentences to communicate. A typical letter to her parents might run on for two pages, but now that she was acknowledging someone new and important in her life, she couldn't think. On a second sheet of paper she began listing stray thoughts about Willy, anything that came into her head. Amused, she put aside the letter to her parents. The list reminded her of magazines for young women, the kind of thing she'd read when she was fifteen. Maybe she was being silly, but how often did that happen? Her list, she thought, could be sandwiched between "Dating Do's and Don'ts" and practical advice on how to treat those pesky yeast infections. Under the heading *Willy* she wrote:

Makes me laugh
Doesn't shave on weekends
Is generous
Can't keep his hands off me (!)
Drinks and smokes—too much of both
Has long scar on heel of foot—right or left?
Likes every kind of fruit, but oranges best
Calls me "pal"

Sleeps on back and side, never on stomach
Is a bad singer—which is good—because I don't sound rotten in comparison
Has curious nature, always asking somebody something
Likes to cook, which lets me off hook

And that's where she had stopped and decided a surprise was in order. She'd buy Willy flowers and do the cooking herself this weekend.

Vee heard the phone ringing while still climbing the stairs to the apartment. She rushed to the front door, managing to unlock it before the caller gave up, and dropped her bags in the hallway.

"Hello?" she said.

"Who's this?"

A man. His voice was unfamiliar, speech slightly slurred. "To whom do you wish to speak?" Vee asked. She looked at the bags sitting on the floor in the hallway. One of them had fallen over on top of the zinnias.

"I want to speak to Willy," the voice said. "Who are you?"

"Willy's at work. Is there a message?"

"There's always a message. And since when does Willy work on Saturday?"

Vee didn't reply.

"Anybody home?" the voice said.

"If you leave your name and number," Vee said, enunciating fiercely, "I'll have Willy return your call."

"The name's Turner. He's got the number. Who are you?"

"Turner?" she said. She knew Turner, or rather knew *of* Turner from a couple of stories Willy had told. Turner had been a roommate of Willy's during college. He was some sort of eccentric, Vee supposed, though Willy had once described him as a "wise guy drunk genius." She hoped Willy wasn't often given to bursts of bad Beat poetry.

"Calling all cars," Turner said.

"What?"

"I thought I had lost you."

Vee introduced herself and tried to breathe some warmth into her voice, which wasn't easy, considering Turner's phone manner.

"So *you're* the latest girlfriend," Turner exclaimed. "Tell Willy I called." And then he hung up, good-bye Turner.

Vee looked at the receiver in her hand. *A sensitive soul,* she told herself.

She gathered the groceries from the floor and took them to the kitchen. The zinnias were crushed, beyond saving. She tossed them in the trash and put the lilacs in water. On the kitchen table she spotted the list she'd made in the morning. She picked up a pen, and beneath *Likes to cook, which lets me off hook,* she wrote, *Has rude insinuating friend—could be trouble.*

17 · *Lunch with Augie*

Willy said, "I don't get it. Two men jump from the *Nora* the minute the ship berths. Why is that a problem? The captain's the one who has to replace the men."

Augie Thom finished his first vodka martini and another was brought to the table. He still hadn't looked at the menu, which lay in his lap.

"What if the captain made a phone call?" Augie said. "What if he called U.S. Immigration?"

"Did this happen?"

"Let's say an hour ago. Let's say I would have phoned but we were meeting for lunch anyway."

Willy watched the ice melt at the bottom of his glass. Twice a month he met Augie Thom for lunch and they talked business. Augie talked, Willy mostly listened. Augie represented the longshoremen on Pier 18, the dock where the steamship agency's inbound cargo was unloaded.

Willy said, "So the captain called Immigration. I still don't understand why two men deserting ship should concern the steamship agency. We arrange to have cargo moved from one place to another. We take care of the documentation, have stowage plans distributed to your men, make sure everything we handle gets cleared through customs. But crew members who desert, that's somebody else's headache."

"Could be our headache," Augie said. "Yours and mine."

"I don't see it."

"When Immigration gets word of crew members jumping ship and entering the country illegally—only a couple of minutes after it's happened, remember—they move very fast and they don't take chances. What they do is seal the pier."

"*Seal* the pier? You mean the pier's sealed right now?"

"It's happened before. Some guy jumps ship, but instead of making a run for it maybe he hides out for a while. You know how big the warehouse is. Maybe he breaks into one of the containers my men have already unloaded. Maybe he wedges himself between stacked bags of cashews or haricot beans, who knows. He could be anywhere."

"Wait a second," Willy said. "Are your men unloading right now?"

"They've got a job to do."

"Wait a second. If the pier's sealed, then none of the cargo coming off the *Nora* can be delivered."

Augie didn't answer.

"And what about the truckers I've arranged to come pick up cargo?" Willy said.

"Can't get inside a sealed pier."

"Then why are you unloading? I've got thirty-four tons of lamb from Auckland that's supposed to go from a reefer chamber in the ship's hold to a refrigerated trailer. Jesus. You're telling me that meat's sitting on the dock?"

"You see the problem?"

Willy pushed away the fresh whiskey and soda that had just been brought to the table. He'd ordered it, but now wasn't so sure he ought to be drinking. Augie was more than halfway through his second vodka martini.

"How long can Immigration keep the pier sealed?" Willy asked.

"Long as they like. Once we were sealed for a day and a half. Some Filipino jumped and made it all the way down to Disneyland while Immigration was still sniffing around the pier. Guy was only caught because the Disney people wouldn't let him in. I guess he didn't look right."

"Back up a second. I still don't know why my meat's on the dock."

"In a case like this *all* your cargo would be on the dock."

"I don't care about the other cargo. The other stuff won't spoil. Why is the meat on the dock?"

"You think the longshoremen only work for your agency? We've got outbound cargo that has to be loaded. My men discharge cargo marked San Francisco, they load cargo tagged to leave port. The *Nora*'s scheduled to sail at four this afternoon, and if she isn't loaded by then I'm fucked. Keep that in mind. At six-twenty-five I got a second ship due to berth. Not one of yours, one being handled by another agency. If the pier was sealed when the second ship was due to arrive, the second ship would be diverted somewhere else, some other pier."

"Meaning what?"

"Meaning my men would be out of half a day's work. Meaning fucked again, what do you think? These guys are paid by the hour, they count on overtime. Two ships to unload and load, that's a sixteen-hour day. They need the money. I don't have another ship scheduled to berth at the pier until Thursday, which means a lot of my men don't work until then. No ship, no work. They expect me to keep the pier running, that's my job. You understand now? You understand how we both could have a problem? I think so."

Augie finished his second vodka martini and a third was brought to the table. Willy pushed his own whiskey and soda still farther away.

Augie said, "So in a case like this, listen to me, Willy, in a case like this we could use a solution. You're a hot-shit inbound freight manager, maybe you can think of something."

"I'm not sure getting smashed before lunch is going to help us much."

Augie ignored the remark. "How do you open a sealed pier? Let's try and figure this out. There's got to be all kinds of ways. Last time this happened to me, this was five years ago, I tried a bribe. I gave a hundred-dollar bill to each Immigration officer searching the pier. Four officers, four hundred bucks. That was a mistake. It only took one of them to snitch, then we all got caught in the shitstorm. The union suspended me ninety days, but you know what? When I came back I was a hero, the men loved me. Longshoremen all over the city were buying me drinks. They didn't care I was offering bribes. They only saw I was trying to keep the pier open and everybody working."

"The agency could get its ass sued if that meat spoils," Willy said.

"So think of something."

"I'm thinking. I'm also wondering why you don't look worried. You're on your third drink, you haven't ordered lunch yet."

"I've got confidence in you, Willy. You've been with the steamship agency what, three years?"

"Almost two."

"And how long ago was it they made you a hot-dick manager?"

"Last February. You already know that."

"You see how fast things happen? Everybody says you got your eyes open, you'll think of something."

"Should I be thinking legal or illegal? Just so I know."

"Don't worry about legal or illegal. Find the solution first."

Willy had a taste of the whiskey and soda and put it back on the table at arm's length. If the drink sat right in front of him he'd sip and sip and not even know it until the glass was empty. He had an idea, though, the glimmer of a plan, and talked it out as it came to him.

"What if I were to make a phone call?" he said.

Augie leaned forward, catching the menu that slid from his lap.

"What if I were to call you at the pier and identify myself as someone from the police department?"

"Go on."

"I say I've picked up the two guys who've skipped. Do we have their names?"

"You can always get the names from the crew list. Very simple. But how come the police know these guys have skipped? Why were they picked up?"

"What if they'd been drinking?"

"They can get drunk on ship."

Another measured sip from the whiskey and soda. "All right," Willy said. "I say they got picked up in a stolen car. They were desperate."

"Much better. What part would I play in this?"

"You relay the information to the Immigration officer in charge on the pier."

"Not so good. Whoever the guy is, no one from Immigration is going to trust me after the bribe business five years ago. If you're police, the guy in charge is going to want to talk to you directly. He'll want to know where you're holding the jumpers. He'll want to see them right away. If you're SFPD, he can hop in his car and be at the Department of Justice in about ten minutes. If you're lucky he opens the pier as he leaves, but before you know it he's back again, mad as hell, wanting to crack somebody's nut."

"So I'm not the police. How about highway patrol? I'm a state trooper. I've picked up two guys in a stolen vehicle."

"Vehicle's a good cop word. What highway?"

Willy already had it. "101, down near San Jose. I've brought them to station headquarters along the highway there. How far is that from here?"

"Fifty miles or so. San Jose is good. That would tie them up for a while."

Another tug on the whiskey and soda. Willy was feeling better as the plan put on detailed weight. "And, Augie, you know in your office down on the pier there, you've got that conference box hooked up to the phone?"

Augie nodded.

"As soon as I call, you put me on hold and get the Immigration officer, the guy in charge. He'll be around?"

"He'd probably be in the warehouse searching for the jumpers. Him and the rest of his men."

"You call him over, call them all over, say you've got a state trooper on the line. When they get to your office you flip on the conference box so everybody can listen. This way I'm not talking to the Immigration guy directly, I'm talking to several people at once, they're all hearing me tell the story. You can get the names of the guys that skipped?"

"I already told you."

"Will they be carrying identification?"

"All crew members carry passports and papers. The information's included on the crew list. What you'd do is read their names and passport numbers over the box. Five minutes is all it would take to say everything. Three minutes. Only you'd have to be sure Immigration understood you were holding the men down there in San Jose. They want the jumpers, they'll have to make the pickup."

"Would that one call be enough to break the seal on the pier?"

"That would do it," Augie said. "Long as you make your call from an outside booth, I don't see how anyone could prove what you were up to."

"What *we* were up to."

Augie nodded again, only now directed a slaphappy grin towards what remained of his third drink.

"Did I say something funny?" Willy said.

"I'm getting hungry. Maybe we better order."

Willy waved his arm, dismissing drinks, lunch, everything but the problem in front of them. "Have I missed something?"

Augie held open a hand. "The pier's not sealed," he said.

"What are you talking about?"

"Nobody jumped from the *Nora*. I wanted to see what sort of solution you'd hit on if you thought the pier was sealed."

"This has been an exercise?"

Augie said yes, something like an exercise.

"A game over drinks before the prawns or red snapper or whatever it is we're going to order for lunch?" Willy said.

"Not a game. In this business you learn to expect problems. Everyday problems, they don't surprise you, it's part of the job. You know what I mean. But major fuck-ups, that's something else. For them you've got to be ready. Sealing the pier is a major. Everybody's affected—your agency, longshoremen, consignees of cargo. It happened five years ago, I told you, and it's going to happen again. When it does, I want to have a plan, a fast way to get the pier open again. You just gave me another plan. It's not legal, but it's cleaner than a bribe."

"What do you mean another plan? You've got others?"

"Depending on the situation. There are plenty of reasons for sealing a pier. Maybe somebody's smuggling drugs, maybe cargo's getting pilfered. You want to order lunch or not?"

"I thought we had a crisis here."

"What if we had? Now I know I can count on you."

"And what about you? You pull something like this, a stunt, I don't know."

"Not a stunt," Augie corrected. "Listen to this. I got my union card right out of high school. Big deal, I know, but you've got to understand the card still means something. I've been on the docks twenty-three years. I've been running Pier 18 nine years. I'm a regular guy, I buy American, my men trust me. You don't think you can count on me, go fuck your mother."

Willy gave it up then. He drained off his whiskey and soda while Augie went to the bathroom.

"So how's the abalone in this place?" Willy finally said. He'd been studying the menu.

Augie made a circle with his thumb and forefinger. "That's what I'm having. Delicious. You want another pop with the meal?"

Why not, Willy thought.

18 · *The Museum*

When at last the field had been narrowed to three, Vee was invited back to the museum for a final interview. She was in competition for the job as assistant curator of antiquities.

The director was seated behind a massive desk in his office when Vee walked in. His name was Rasmussen, and he was a tall man somewhere in his fifties who dressed indifferently and spoke easily. Vee sat across from him in a green leather armchair studded with brass. A club chair, she thought. The kind of chair in which you relaxed. She didn't feel relaxed. Whenever she shifted her body the leather cushion she was sitting upon exhaled air.

The two other candidates for the job, both men, were already employed in antiquities departments with museums back east. One in Buffalo, the other in Richmond, Virginia. And though they were both young, in fact not much older than Vee, they had, the director told her, seven years of museum experience between them.

Vee crossed her legs and smoothed the wrinkle in her skirt, though underneath she could feel her slip was still bunched. She wanted to stand and straighten herself. And what did *seven years of museum experience between them* mean, anyway?

Were the two men going to be hired in tandem? Tag-team curators?

During the course of the interview Rasmussen picked up a bronze axhead that had been pinning down a pile of paper on his desk top. The object was no more than six or seven inches in length, though from the way he held it, first in one hand, then the other, Vee could see it was heavy. Ancient Luristan, she thought, the identification of objects by now reflexive, a trained habit, almost a tic. The blade of the axhead emerged from the gaping jaws of a fantastically imagined lion, while a row of blunt spikes ran along the back of the head and down the bronze shaft.

"Both of these men have published," Rasmussen was saying. "One of them spent a year on an important dig in Sardinia."

Why was he telling her these things? Had she been summoned a second time, having already *dreamed* about the job, only to be told she'd been found wanting? Rasmussen knew she was fresh from school. He knew she needed another three months to finish writing her dissertation.

Over the phone, just a couple of days ago, he'd explained why he was inviting her back to the museum. She was a woman, that was the first thing. Vee didn't blanch when Rasmussen said this. She didn't care how she got the job. Similar institutions, the better ones anyway, already had women on staff. Not as secretaries, not in the registrar's office, but on curatorial staff. It was time this museum caught up.

Another thing. Vee had started out as a painter, not as a student of buried cultures, and as a painter had achieved modest success before changing fields. Rasmussen found this meaningful. Vee didn't argue.

And then something else, more compelling than reasons one or two. During her previous interview Vee hadn't inquired about salary or benefits. She hadn't inquired at all. What she wanted to know was the size of the department's budget and the ratio of donated objects to objects purchased with museum funds. She had a list of questions. She wanted to know if there was a procedure for soliciting gifts from collectors. She wanted to know who was responsible for promotion and how the museum kept the public curious and coming back for repeat visits.

These were not academic questions. These were questions none of the other candidates had asked.

Now Rasmussen said, "I still haven't come to a decision," though he hardly looked pained or discomfited at the prospect of having to make a choice. The axhead was still in his hands, passing absently from one palm to the other. In fact he appeared so self-assured, so composed in his padded swivel chair behind his giant desk, axhead in hand, that Vee guessed he'd either already made up his mind or he was waiting for her to make up his mind for him.

"May I?" she said, hand held forward.

The director passed her the axhead. His smile was encouraging. "What do you make of it?"

"Luristan," Vee said, eyes on the object. "Fifteen hundred B.C., maybe earlier."

"Yes, but what do you make of it?"

Vee lay the axhead in the flat of her lap and began sifting through her handbag for her pocket magnifier. She'd been self-conscious when she'd first bought the magnifier, thinking it a pretense, a professional accessory of marginal value. But now the lens enlarged the heavy bronze, making visible what had been indefinite or hidden.

She took more time than she really needed. The object was wrong, either an outright forgery or a damaged piece that had been doctored. The casting of the bronze was relatively crisp, which proved nothing, but the patina—a striking sea green— was too uniform, too consistent, as if set overnight in a pail of acids and tinted paint. Ancient bronzes more often exhibited a random patchy surface that varied not only in color and tone but in texture as well. Tiny islands of red cuprite should be visible under a lens. But the magnifier picked up only flatness and opacity. The object was static, without depth or the breath of life. And if the patina was wrong, the bronze itself was suspect.

"Is this from the museum's collection?" Vee asked.

"A very recent donation," the director said, "though we haven't really accepted it yet. I've told the donor we want a couple of weeks to examine the object. This is routine, something we do with all of our gifts, big or small."

"What are you going to tell him?"

"I was hoping you'd tell me."

All right, she was being tested. Counterfeit or not, the axhead was serving a real purpose. She put the magnifier back in her handbag and hesitated a moment before taking out a small bottle of nail polish remover. Sometimes she wore polish on her toes. For one reason or another, Willy was stirred by the sight of painted toenails. Ardor so simple to rouse seemed mean to deny. Then again, painting her nails was a favor she could always withhold to express her dissatisfaction. It occurred to her, sitting in Rasmussen's office in the middle of an important interview, that she hadn't painted her nails for several weeks.

"Vee?" the director said.

She held the bottle of remover in the flat of her hand, label up and easy to read. "We could always run a test," she said. Like rubbing alcohol or half a dozen other solvents, nail polish remover quickly dissolved many false patinas.

"That won't be necessary," Rasmussen said. "I can see you're not happy with the piece."

She dropped the bottle into her handbag and then placed the axhead on the edge of the director's desk, distancing herself from the suspect bronze. She wondered what else she might say when she suddenly realized the authenticity of the object might be beside the point.

She said, "How important is the donor to the museum?"

Rasmussen leaned forward, the cuff of his shirt shooting from his suit sleeve, and retrieved the axhead.

"He gave us a Byzantine bronze mirror last year. Nothing very special, but we wanted to encourage him. Several months ago I was invited to his house for dinner. Before eating we walked through the downstairs rooms and he showed me his collection. He's got some wonderful things. Roman marbles, Minoan seals and pots, more than a dozen Apulian terracottas. . . ."

Vee sensed she was on track. "If I was with the Antiquities Department . . ." she began.

"Yes?"

". . . I'd accept the axhead."

"Even if it was wrong?"

"Maybe whether it's right or wrong doesn't matter. The object isn't important enough to worry about. I'd accept it as a gift, then bury it in storage."

"And why would you do that?"

"To keep the gifts coming. The integrity of the museum isn't going to be damaged by owning a minor forgery. No one says you have to exhibit the piece."

Rasmussen nodded, seemed to think, his lips drawn in on themselves. Then he took a ring of keys from the middle drawer of his desk and excused himself, heels clacking against waxed linoleum once he reached the hallway beyond his office door.

He was gone ten minutes, and when he returned he carried a pair of ribbed lavender cups.

"I got these from one of the display cases," he said.

Another test, Vee thought. She lifted one of the delicate cups from the desk and studied it with her pocket magnifier. Opaque glass, minute chipping along the rim and disk foot, but otherwise in excellent condition, the glass body remarkably well preserved and fresh. She found no deep surface abrasion that might indicate overzealous cleaning, though random scratches—a sign of normal wear and tear—were visible. Perhaps the cups had been sealed in a vacuum. That happened sometimes. Two thousand years in an airtight container and objects emerged as if from a time capsule. But where had the cups originated? When were they crafted? She counted ribs. One, two, three, twelve in all. She estimated the cup's diameter. Two and three-quarter inches. She was stalling. Ancient glass was her no-man's-land, a field she'd neglected to really study. You couldn't cover everything. Carved stone was her first love and came easily. Earthenware and bronze she could usually figure out given the time. But glass? The cup looked alien, a mystery, worlds removed from the dismissed axhead.

"Having trouble?" the director said.

"Give me another minute." Trying to concentrate and be polite at the same time was impossible.

"What about the time frame?"

"I wouldn't even want to guess. A lot more glass from the ancient world has survived than was first suggested, I remember reading that, but I've never seen anything like this. It's so fresh. I really don't know where to begin."

"Try the twentieth century."

Vee's gaze jerked from the cup in her lap. Rasmussen was sliding open one of the drawers to his desk. He was clutching a bottle of wine by the neck and beginning to dig through yet another drawer.

"Nineteen twenty-five," he said cheerfully. "Art Deco. These cups were made for the Exposition Internationale in Paris. Here we go." He held up a T-shaped corkscrew with a wooden handle.

Vee faked a smile. She'd been had. The wine on the desk was a California Zinfandel.

"I don't understand," she said, meaning not only the ribbed cups and the bottle of wine but *all* of it, the entire interview.

"I was just having some last-minute fun," Rasmussen confessed. "I couldn't resist. I want you to consider yourself hired, Vee. Congratulations." He held out his hand.

So the ribbed cups were a prank, and the Zinfandel the reward for having survived the final cut and being a good sport. She was finally employed, she was *on staff*. He must have decided he was going to hire her before he'd left the office to fetch the cups from the display case. She had the job, she'd outmaneuvered the two other candidates with their *seven years of experience between them*.

"I expect you're pleased," Rasmussen said.

"Very much." Vee accepted the cup of wine and sipped with both hands, trying to collect herself. "But we still have something to discuss." She took another sip.

"Fire away." He poured more wine with a steady hand.

"My salary," Vee said. "We've got to figure out how much the museum can afford to pay me."

19 · *The Alibi*

Willy loosened the knot in his tie and thumbed open his collar. The air inside the office of the steamship agency felt close and used, already exhaled, better suited for hothouse tomatoes. He looked at the clock on the wall and decided to eat.

The office lunchroom was all but deserted when he sat down at one of the round tables and peeled sticky plastic wrap from the tuna sandwich he'd bought on his way to work in the morning. He thought he'd eat quickly and then read the *Chronicle.*

But if Willy wanted to eat and read and be by himself, why did he pick the only table in the lunchroom occupied by another person? He looked at the secretary on the other side of the table and tried to remember her name, a mental search akin to flipping through a desktop Rolodex. Susan? Sarah? He'd seen her sitting at a keyboard in the telex room, seen her taking long strides down the hallway. Sometimes she filled in for the office receptionist.

Sally, he told himself.

Her lunch consisted of celery sticks and radishes and a container of cottage cheese. She looked up and smiled politely as Willy unwrapped his sandwich.

Sally was wearing a sleeveless cotton print dress that left a broad patch of her chest exposed, yet the dress was really more

sensible than provocative. With the summer heat and the ab-
sence of air-conditioning, everyone in the office had taken to
wearing the bare white-collar minimum.

While making small talk with Sally—the rumored cost-of-
living increase they hoped to get by the end of the month—he
admired her bright red hair and green eyes. A band of freckles
ran across her chest, disappearing into the cleavage between
her breasts and then out again. The freckles emphasized her
lack of color while oddly enhancing her appearance of fitness
and good health. She was twenty-two and looked wonderful.
Willy said as much and Sally blushed. She confided that though
her boyfriend was great, just a terrific guy in so many ways, he
wasn't very fond of freckles, particularly the ones on her chest.

The man must have his head up his ass, Willy thought.

Conversation returned to small talk—another leap from the
Golden Gate Bridge, Sally had heard a report on the radio—yet
the tone of the talk became more intimate and somehow con-
spiratorial. Willy suggested they finish their lunch hour in the
park at Union Square, just a couple of blocks from the office.

Sally's boyfriend, with whom she lived, was deep into middle age and twice divorced. He worked as a lobbyist for the fruit
and vegetable growers in the Imperial Valley and had recently
taken to carrying a denim briefcase. He spent much of his time
at the state capitol, and only that morning had called from his
motel room in Sacramento to say he wouldn't be returning
home until the following day. This happened regularly and no
longer bothered Sally as much as she thought it should. Willy
listened and nodded and said nothing of Vee. He was entranced
by Sally's skin, by the bean-brown freckles inscribed on her
chest.

They sat on a solid-cast concrete bench beneath a eucalyptus
tree in the park. The tree's fragrance thickened the air. Willy
was looking off in the distance at the pigeons perched on the
window ledge of an office building when he found himself
asking Sally, in a voice that didn't sound to him like his own,
if she'd like to get a drink after work. "Since you're going to be
alone," he said.

Sally didn't drink, never had, but to Willy's surprise she countered his offer with an invitation of her own. She'd already taken chicken out of the freezer that morning and had been planning, with her boyfriend, to have a barbecue in the backyard. Nothing special, just a midweek summer meal. "It's too hot to cook in the house," she said.

Sally lived across the San Francisco–Oakland Bay Bridge in the Berkeley Hills. Willy followed her in his own car back to her place after work, and right away, almost too quickly, they began preparing dinner. While Sally marinated chicken in the kitchen, Willy wandered out to the backyard, amid bleached grass and rhododendrons, and filled the hibachi with charcoal.

"Where's the lighter fluid?" he shouted from outside.

She didn't hear him.

Back in the kitchen he found her slicing a cucumber on a wooden cutting block next to the sink. Willy walked up behind her and gave her a kiss, a peck really, on the nape of the neck.

Sally twisted around and returned the peck.

Stooping over, he kissed her beautifully freckled chest, then looked into her face, into her green eyes, for a reaction. Sally blushed and gently pushed his head back to where it had been. Slowly, and with great deliberateness, Willy unbuttoned the top of the dress and nuzzled his face against her breasts. Sally's nipples stiffened and she began to lightly sway from the caressing as if keeping time to a silent rhythm in her head. She could have been wearing earphones. Willy's hand, meanwhile, sank like a diver and swam beneath the cotton print dress, then climbed the inside of Sally's thigh. As his middle finger slid beneath the leg band of her panties she whispered, "Let's go to the other room."

They sat on a sofa upholstered with heavy woolen broadcloth, which was hot and itchy and all wrong. Almost immediately Sally got up and went to the linen closet in the hallway and came back with a folded sheet. Her dress was now unbuttoned to the navel, her breasts spilling free. While Sally dropped to her knees and smoothed out the cool sheet on top of the carpet beside the sofa, Willy stood and unbuckled his belt. His zipper sounded extraordinarily loud to him as he opened his pants.

"Wait a sec," Sally whispered.

She took two steps on her knees and slid Willy's pants down his legs, then brought her mouth to him for just a moment. As her head bobbed gently up and down, Willy slipped the sleeveless summer dress from her shoulders. Her back was aswarm with freckles.

He left before the charcoal was even lit, apologizing for having to be somewhere else. He was not specific. In any case Sally didn't protest. That afternoon he'd called Vee at the museum and explained he'd be home a little late, that he was meeting a few people from the office for a drink after work. As he pulled up in front of his apartment house back in San Francisco and searched for a spot to park the car, he remembered the alibi he'd given to Vee over the phone. How could he pretend to have been drinking with friends when he didn't have alcohol on his breath?

He parked the car, walked three blocks east to an old man's bar called Riordan's, a place that served forty-cent drafts, and downed in rapid succession a glass of beer, two shots of whiskey, and then a second glass of beer. Vee would be working on her dissertation now, seated at the card table they'd set up in the living room by the window, wearing her reading glasses and maybe drinking iced tea. Of course he wouldn't tell her what he'd been doing. Confession was an admission of guilt, and that was not at all what he felt. Cheating on Vee hadn't threatened his attachment to her. This was encouraging. This was good news, at least to Willy. Vee would think otherwise, she'd be furious, but then Vee wouldn't know. Discretion would be Willy's shield, alcohol his cover. Though Sally had pleased his senses, loving Vee was becoming a way of life that embodied more than pleasure. Fidelity was not part of this package, this embodiment, not quite yet, though he could see himself slowly drifting in that direction.

He paid for his drinks and left Riordan's feeling hungry. It was eight o'clock. He'd been inside the bar approximately ten minutes. By the time he reached the apartment and greeted Vee his bladder was full.

20 · *Fool's Gold*

She poked her head out from the dark of a recessed doorway and looked up and down the sidewalk. No one in sight. Both sides of the street were lined with parked cars but there was no moving traffic. She stepped out from the sheltered doorway and onto the open walk, her body made ghostly by moonlight.

There was something she had to find. Something of value. She'd know when she found it. She stepped off the curb and passed between two parked cars when her bare foot kicked against something hard. A bottle inside a paper bag skittered across the asphalt. She went after the bag and picked it up and peered inside. An empty pint of cherry wine. She unscrewed the metal cap and sniffed and pulled her face away sharply. This wasn't what she was looking for. She put the bottle back where it had been lying between the parked cars. She was conscious of her naked body, but she didn't feel shame. She looked up and down the street, not hurrying, past parked cars and bagged garbage. The street was deserted. She looked up at the long row of apartment buildings, first one side of the street, then the other, when she saw movement, just a flicker, a hand parting a curtain. Somebody was up there. In a second-story window, in an apartment that looked like her own, that *was* her own, somebody was watching.

"Vee," Willy said. His voice was husky from sleep. "What are you doing at the window?"

"I think I was dreaming," she said. "I was looking for something in the street out here. I don't remember what it was, but I had to find it. For some reason I wasn't wearing clothes. And Willy, when I looked up at our apartment I saw somebody standing in the window."

"It was just a dream. Come back to bed."

"But I was out there for a reason. I was looking for something."

"Maybe if you come back to bed and go to sleep again you'll find it." He patted the mattress.

"Wait a second, I see something out there. Come here, I see something."

Willy got out of bed. The digital clock on the dresser read 3:17.

"Over there," Vee said. "Do you see what I see?"

Both sides of the street were lined with parked cars. After seven in the evening an open space was hard to find.

"Where?"

"By the blue car there. What is that? Is that a Datsun? There. Over *there*. The one without hubcaps. Do you see the car I mean?"

"The Toyota. I see it."

"Now look by the front tire."

"I see something shiny. Something very small and yellow, brassy."

"Gold," Vee said. "It looks like gold, doesn't it? In my dream I was looking for something valuable."

"You're thinking too much about your job at the museum. The night is for sleeping, Vee. For getting a good rest."

"In a minute. I'm going down there to see what that thing is." She grabbed the sheer nightgown by the foot of the bed and slipped it over her head.

"At least put on some shoes."

"I wasn't wearing shoes in the dream."

"You weren't wearing any clothes either."

"Just give me two minutes. I'll be right back."

He heard her descend the hallway stairs, and then from below he heard the heavy front door in the lobby scrape against the tile floor. The door always swelled in the heat.

Vee poked her head out beyond the entrance to the apartment house and looked up and down the sidewalk. No one in sight. She stepped out and passed between two parked cars and crossed the street. The small glittering flat object she'd seen from the window was by the front tire of the blue Toyota. She bent over to scoop up the prize and hurried back to the building.

As she climbed the stairs to the second floor she held the object in her closed fist. Willy was waiting for her on the landing.

"It's a good thing it's the middle of the night," he joked. He could see her shape beneath the sheer nightgown as she mounted the stairs. She was scowling. "What did you find?"

Vee opened her palm. "Beer-bottle cap," she said flatly. "Miller High Life. Probably one of yours."

21 · *Happy Hour*

5:16 Willy was settled on a padded leather stool at the bar. He'd driven straight from the office. This was Friday, time to relax before going home to meet Vee. He took a long pull on his whiskey and soda and glanced at the Johnny Walker promotional clock on the wall. Happy hour lasted until six. Two drinks for the price of one. Ya-hoo. He peeled the red cellophane strip from a fresh pack of cigarettes and almost leisurely patted his pockets for a book of matches.

5:22 Augie Thom appeared in the doorway, silhouetted against daylight. He spotted Willy and hurried over.

"A vodka martini," he told the bartender, adjusting himself on a stool. "Rocks and a twist." He turned to Willy. "So what's on your mind you couldn't tell me over the phone?"

"I thought you might like a drink," Willy said.

"I'd like a couple, but you said you had something to discuss. 'We better meet somewhere,' you said. 'I don't trust the phones.' "

Willy began bobbing his head, unable to conceal his pleasure. "Guess I had you going."

Augie finished his martini in a swallow and chewed on a piece of ice. "What are you getting at?"

"Remember that business about the sealed pier?"

Augie caught the ball. "Tit for tat, is that it? Okay, so maybe I deserve it. But now that you've got me here, how about buying a round?"

"You're ready?"

"I'm waiting."

5:55 Willy eyed the Johnny Walker clock on the wall. "We better get another while the price is right," he said.

"Bartender," Augie commanded.

6:31 Willy and Augie were in conversation. Dominick the bartender was nearby, wiping the bar top with a wet folded rag. He wore a black bow tie and white shirt, a silver nameplate pinned to the breast of his red vest. Drink orders had slowed down in the last half-hour.

"Why don't you ask Dominick?" Augie was saying. "I've never been in this bar before. Every place is different."

Willy was chewing on a swizzle stick. "Hey Dom," he said. He'd introduced himself after the last round. "Augie and I have a question. What do you do when a customer's had too much to drink? In some bars they've got bouncers and the guy's thrown in the street. Other places the bartender's this big bear and *he* throws the guy out."

Dominick stood five feet seven, weighed maybe 120 pounds, and was close to fifty. His hair was gray, his hands small. Clearly he wasn't going to do any throwing. Willy had meant no offense, he was simply curious. This particular bar had the ambience of a club. Dark wood and brass predominated. The tables and chairs looked heavy, the ashtrays were thick.

"So what's the policy?" Willy asked.

Dominick had been listening politely, eyes blinking as Willy spoke. Now he made his face blank and turned stiffly on his heels.

"What'd I say?" Willy whispered. "It was an easy question."

Augie shook his head. They watched Dominick at the far end of the bar. He appeared to be counting ice cubes. Several minutes passed before he returned.

"I thought I'd show you how we do it," Dominick said, giving Willy a wink. "When a customer gets difficult because he's had too much to drink, we stop speaking to him. That's first. After that we walk away from where he's sitting. And after that," he said, bending closer and beginning to smile, "we pretend he doesn't exist."

6:58 Another round, Augie's turn.

7:29 "Do me again, Dom. And one for Augie here."

"I might get going," Augie said, though he stayed where he was.

Dominick snatched their glasses, dumped the melted ice beneath the bar top in one smooth move, and mixed fresh drinks.

"This one's on the house, gentlemen."

8:00 Willy bought Dominick a drink. Actually a phantom drink. Dominick subtracted the price of a whiskey and soda from Willy's ten and put the money in a glass beer mug by the cash register.

"Thank you," Dominick said. Then he went off to wait on another customer.

"I thought he might do that," Augie said. "Some places, you buy the barkeep a drink, he drinks it. That's how it used to be."

"In the olden days, huh? Probably can't drink on duty."

"What is he, a cop?"

"Maybe he doesn't want a drink," Willy said. "Who knows? Dominick's a good bartender. Very attentive, yet he lets us be. Domino, my man." He rapidly drummed his fingers on the bar top, a sudden solo. "I may come back to this place. . . ."

Augie had only been half-listening when he nudged Willy in

the side. "Look at that," he said. "You see the guy in the corner over there?"

"The guy by himself?"

"That's him. Look at that. Regular suit, tie, he's got a brief-case by his foot there."

"So?"

"Look closer, past the clothes, the office job. What do you see?"

"He looks lonely, sad, I don't know."

"He's sad all right. That guy's been on a controlled binge for years, guaranteed."

"How can you tell?"

"You can tell. The red face, the puffiness, the way he knocks them back without flinching, like all he's doing is breathing. He's had a few."

"So have we."

"But not all of them in fifteen minutes, Willy. I've been watching this guy since he came in. I know the type. He's not having fun or socializing, you can bet on that. What he's doing is hard time. I get very nervous when I see people like that."

"A simple solution, Aug, and your problem is solved."

"What's that?"

"Don't look."

"Don't look?"

Willy nodded, then spun on his stool and took in the bar-room. "This place could use some music, you know?" He drummed his fingers on his thighs. "A jukebox would go a long way."

8:19 "How about another?" Willy said.

"I should be shoving off."

"One more, Augie, a quick one, no big deal. We can switch to beer if you want."

Augie looked at the Johnny Walker clock and sighed. "I bet-ter call the wife, then. I've been in the shithouse before. I all but *built* the shithouse, believe me."

"A tough guy like you, Augie?" Keeping it light.

"You don't know much, do you? I forget I'm in a bar with somebody half my age."

"Not half," Willy said. He ordered two beers from Dominick.

"Like I'm drinking with my fucking son," Augie continued. "Don't you have a wife or girlfriend, somebody to call?"

"I called from the office, said I'd be a little late."

"You're *already* a little late."

"She'll understand."

"Don't kid yourself," Augie said. "You have some change I can use for the phone?"

8:51 "The *Princesa* is berthing late Sunday night," Augie said. As he got off the bar stool he hitched up his pants. "She's carrying mango and papaya and banana, and she's running half a day late. We're going to have to do some fancy dancing to get her unloaded and back on schedule. You'll be down at the pier first thing Monday with the documents?"

Willy said yes, finished his beer. "One more, Aug. One for the open road, for the high seas."

"No, I'm leaving. Give it a rest, Willy, you've got the whole weekend. Don't you have somewhere to be?"

"One more, a *final* round, and then I'll walk out with you. Where the hell's Dominick? There he is."

"See you Monday, Willy."

"Come on, Augie, don't be a goddamn baby."

"You're calling me a baby? A squirt like you, punk in a button-down shirt, you got the juice to call me a baby?"

"Yup."

"All right, order me another while I hit the john. *One*, that's it."

Willy hailed Dominick while Augie was gone and made special arrangements for the last round. He laid a twenty-dollar bill on the bar and watched Dominick fill a one-gallon stainless-steel ice bucket with beer from the tap. Augie's last drink. This was going to be good. Dominick then neatly filled a shot glass from the same tap. Willy's drink.

The best practical jokes, Willy reflected as he lit another

cigarette, are born in bars when you're half-skunked. Even Dominick seemed to be having fun.

But Augie would have none of it and just shook his head. "You don't know when to quit, do you?" he said to Willy.

"You agreed to have one more, Aug. Honor the contract."

"A piece of advice," Augie said, pointing a finger. "Never shit a shitter. Remember that."

9:18 Willy was still brooding over Augie's desertion and sat hunched forward, his weight on his elbows. Dominick had finished his shift at nine and was replaced by a man without a name tag who seemed to disapprove of the bucket of beer on the bar top. In any case the man was slow to empty Willy's ashtray and hadn't said hello.

Willy had been dunking his shot glass into the beer bucket when he overheard chattering voices from a table some twenty feet away. Two women were sharing drinks and looking every now and then in his direction. They were dressed well, both in suits, sensible flats, some makeup. Businesswomen, probably. Willy studied their reflection in the mirror behind the bar and then spun around on his stool.

"Would you ladies care to join me for a drink?" he said. He straightened his tie and felt a pleasant stirring between his legs. This is a little like happy hour, he thought. Two for one and all for me.

The prettier of the pair spoke up. "No thanks," she said. "You seem to be doing just fine all by yourself." She then leaned towards her companion and whispered something amusing, for they both began laughing.

Stung, Willy retreated back into his brooding and lit a cigarette. The pack was almost empty. Somewhere, he suspected, the evening had begun to turn. He'd walked into the bar feeling relaxed and happy, and now, four hours later, he was growing ill-tempered. He pushed away the bucket of beer, already warm and disagreeably flat, and ordered a cold bottle of Olympia from the nameless bartender. He could hear the two women chattering. Certain words were clear, though never an entire sentence at a time. *He,* he heard. And *one of those . . . probably drives . . . small wonder . . . soft. . . .*

He was sure they were talking about him. He sucked on the cold Oly, loosened his tie again. *Not likely . . . checking account . . . too much. . . .*

Enough, he thought, impatient at trying to decipher their conversation. He spun around on the stool and stared at the two women until he was certain he had their attention. Then he tilted his head back to get the dregs from his beer, poked his tongue inside the bottle, and ever so slowly licked the rim.

One of the women put a hand to her mouth and stopped talking in mid-sentence.

Willy ordered another beer.

"You wouldn't be bothering those two over there, would you?" asked the bartender.

"What's it to you?" Willy said.

9:47 They were at it again, chattering away, having a grand time, and probably talking about him. Willy felt he had no recourse but to repeat his routine, this time with an even ruder twist. While his tongue lewdly licked and circled the rim of the beer bottle, one of his hands fondled his groin. He was not subtle.

Nor were the women. They briefly conferred, grabbed their purses, and threaded their way between tables until they reached the bar.

"You've got an awfully small tongue," the prettier of the two said to Willy. She spoke sharply, loud enough for other patrons to hear. The bartender began walking towards the commotion.

"Is that so?" Willy said.

The woman nodded solemnly. "You know what they say about men with small tongues, don't you?"

"I'll bite," Willy said. Something was going wrong. "What do they say?"

Instead of answering, the woman drew a bead on Willy's crotch and stared as if her eyes might do damage.

The bartender was the first to break the silence. "Good for you, honey," he said with surprising force. Other voices—from the bar, from nearby tables—lent their support.

Willy imagined a large rough hand reaching out and squeezing his scrotum, never letting go. He held up his arms. "Okay, okay," he said, an ingratiating smile curling his lips. "I can take a joke. . . ."

"Who's joking?" the woman said, addressing Willy's crotch. "A little thing like that, it's nothing to laugh about." The second woman put a hand on Willy's thigh and teasingly raked him with her fingernails. "Must be kind of tough on the girls, huh?"

I've been eaten alive, Willy thought.

9:56 He tried to order another Oly as soon as the women had left, but the bartender lingered down at the far end.

What do you do when a customer's had too much?

10:13 Only after he'd stood and begun sifting through his pockets for car keys did he realize he'd never be able to drive. One more problem. A *major*, Augie might say. He went to the pay phone in the corner by the men's room and dialed his home number.

"Vee?"

"I was expecting you hours ago," she said. She'd answered right away, halfway into the first ring. A bad sign.

"I stayed longer than I'd intended." Making an effort to sound casual, defer the argument until he was safely home. He'd been mauled enough for one night.

"You said you'd be home about seven."

"I did?"

"Just forget it, Willy. You sound drunk. How are you getting home? You better not even think about driving."

"Well of course not. What I was thinking was that you might grab a cab down here and drive us both home."

"You're serious?"

"Yes."

"I'm already home."

"Vee. . . ."

"I've already eaten. *By myself.*"

"Vee. . . ." His throat was dry. An evening of nonstop drinking and his throat was dry. He'd give the last two cigarettes in his pack for a sip of beer.

"Take a cab," Vee was saying. "Leave the car there, you're not helpless."

He'd been fearing this suggestion. "I'm not sure I have enough money." There were three singles and some loose change by his place at the bar, but his wallet was empty. He'd run through something like fifty dollars.

"You've got to be joking."

Who's joking? the woman had said. *A little thing like that, it's nothing to laugh about.*

"Why don't you have enough money?" Vee said. "You had enough to get yourself drunk."

"I misfired. Misfigured, I mean." Jesus. "I mis*calculated.*"

"In more ways than one, Willy. I don't care how you get home, I'm going to bed. You can be a real prick, you know that? Do you?"

He walked away from the phone then, leaving the receiver hanging from its short metal cord. He exited the bar by the side entrance, forfeiting his few last dollars in order to avoid the nameless bartender and customers certain to stare. Once outside he pulled off his suit jacket and folded it into an odd square. He'd sleep in the car, make a bed of the cramped backseat. If any luck was due him, he'd pass out fast.

22 · *Red China*

Vee received a Valentine's Day card in the mail. The card came one day early and was unsigned. In place of a signature, however, was a fiery red heart drawn in lipstick.

Willy? Vee wondered. She decided for the moment to say nothing.

The following day, the fourteenth, a messenger delivered a package to the museum. Vee was at her desk and felt self-conscious as she tore at the wrapping paper. Inside was a one-pound bag of sugar and an attached note, but all the note said was, "Sometimes you're sweet. . . ." No signature, though once again there was a lipstick heart.

Later that same afternoon a second messenger delivered a second package. A bottle of cider vinegar this time, and another note. "Sometimes I'm sour. . . ." And of course a red heart.

Who was sending her cards and packages? Willy was the logical choice, but Vee was still uncertain. That morning he mentioned he'd like to take her out to dinner in the evening. They'd been finishing breakfast and getting ready for work. The radio was on, and in between the news and a weather report the disc jockey made a passing remark about Valentine's Day. Only then had Willy suggested dinner, as if the disc jockey's words had prompted him.

But if not Willy, who? The red lipstick might indicate a woman, though Vee didn't have all that many girlfriends in San Francisco, and none she could think of who might want to remember her on Valentine's Day. There was Steven, of course, a colleague at the museum with whom she'd become friendly. But that was just it, Steven was a *friend*. Whoever was sending her cards and packages and romantic red hearts was intimating more than friendship.

When Vee finally arrived home that evening she found Willy sitting in the kitchen. The stowage plan of a freighter was spread out on the table and Willy was busy shifting pallets of this cargo or that from one hatch to another. Sometimes he brought work home from the office. A bottle of beer, a pocket calculator, and a scratch pad filled with figures were on the table as well.

"I'm just about finished," he said. "Another ten minutes. Why don't you get ready for dinner?"

Vee tossed her handbag on the sofa and went to the bedroom to change, and there on her pillow was a delicate plate of bone china. Drawn in lipstick in the center of the plate was a tiny red heart. A note was there too. "Sometimes you're sweet, sometimes I'm sour. If we were Chinese, we'd make a great dish."

Vee clutched the note and turned, only to discover Willy standing in the bedroom doorway, a silly grin lighting his face. In the palm of his hand was the case of red lipstick.

"So where would you like to eat?" he said.

Vee read the note again before answering. "Chinatown," she said.

23 · *An Open Line*

Always the obligation to respond. The phone rings, you pick up the receiver. Willy had seen this principle in action even on the street. He'd been walking along Van Ness Avenue, past a showroom of sleek Cadillacs behind plate glass, when a phone in a booth on the corner began ringing. A teenage boy just a few brisk steps ahead of Willy looked over at the booth and slowed his pace. There was no one else in the immediate vicinity—just Willy, the boy, the north-south flow of traffic along Van Ness. A pair of sea gulls wheeled in the wind overhead.

"I think it's for you," Willy said. A joke.

But the boy didn't laugh. He stepped into the booth and picked up the receiver and said hello to God knows who. He answered the call. Another line of communication opened for no reason at all.

When the phone rang in Willy's apartment he paused in mid-motion. He'd been on his way out, jacket buttoned and collar upturned, keys to the front door in hand. Should he answer? If the caller was his mother on the other side of the country she'd want to talk for forty-five minutes. If the call was from the steamship agency then surely a problem had developed, cargo without papers, a documentation snag, something requiring a trip down to the pier, which he didn't want to make.

This was Thursday evening, still early, and Willy had run out of cigarettes. He'd been about to go down to the Greek deli on the corner, a five-minute round-trip, when the phone rang. If the caller was his mother he'd *want* a cigarette. Any call at all was made easier by having a pack of cigarettes within reach. The right call just now, the perfect call, would be the wrong one, and if the number was wrong, why answer?

The phone kept ringing, and this told Willy something. People calling locally gave up sooner than people calling long-distance. A long-distance call carried a sense of urgency, regardless of the message. Money was being spent, effort extended, eleven digits required to complete the connection. Even the most frivolous long-distance calls were invested with an importance that local calls lacked. Putting the keys back in his coat pocket, feeling for cigarettes he knew were not there, he went to the phone and lifted the receiver.

Turner on the line. Willy's old buddy, now chief chemist in charge of flavor research for a brewery in El Paso. They talked four, maybe five times a year, always long-distance. Willy had been threatening to visit Turner ever since he got out of college. Someday he'd get around to it. Turner himself made no pretense about visiting Willy in San Francisco. Natural disasters dismayed him. A few years back he'd been offered a job with a rum distillery in Freeport. His own lab, the easy enchantment of life in the Bahamas, a bungalow overlooking the bay provided by the company. A fantasy job. But he turned it down, no regrets, for fear of hurricanes. San Francisco was another place he didn't want to hear about. Earthquake country. The entire state of California made him nervous.

But he wasn't calling to discuss disaster. No talk of tornadoes, of the rashness of people building homes on flood plains. He had good news and wanted to share his joy. He wanted to celebrate. The man was happy.

Had anyone else begun a phone conversation in this manner Willy would have expected one of two things—an impending marriage or the announcement of a birth. Knowing Turner, something else was up.

One night they had driven from Boston to a county fair in southern New Hampshire. The trip took ninety minutes, the May evening was chill but clear. They shared a six-pack of Narragansett along the way, and by the time they arrived night had fallen and the fairgrounds were busy with milling bodies— dairy farmers and high school kids, software specialists who worked along Route 128, small children sucking sno-cones.

They rambled from booth to booth, drinking keg beer from twelve-ounce waxed cups. They saw the fire-eater, the bearded lady, a Shetland pony with two tails. Tired stuff. Willy won a quart of RC Cola by picking off three out of four weighted wooden ducks with a beanbag. Turner had his picture taken with a snake draped over his shoulders. Snakes didn't frighten him.

Over by the dog-racing track Willy spied a blue pitched tent. His senses steered him. A painted sign by the entrance de-picted a larger-than-life beauty with cascading red hair and glittering eyes and hands coyly concealing her treasures. Her costume consisted of hoop earrings and high heels. She looked like Brenda Starr.

Turner wasn't even remotely curious, but Willy bought two tickets and pulled him inside. The tent was still filling with customers. Willy guided Turner to the first row in front of the plywood-platform stage. They waited. When a recording of the Captain and Tennille singing "Love Will Keep Us Together" erupted from a scratchy speaker overhead, a woman appeared from the back of the stage and danced her way forward to within feet of where Willy and Turner stood. She wore a sur-prisingly modest two-piece sequined outfit and a pair of red heels. She looked nothing like the painted lady outside, but within thirty seconds a promise had been fulfilled and her sequined two-piece lay on the stage floor. She was not unat-tractive, though Turner couldn't help pointing out an appen-dectomy scar and observing that the woman's belly was puffy because she was retaining water, probably from the use of an oral contraceptive. These were the last words he spoke the entire evening.

She danced on the edge of the stage, breasts bouncing, her dancing neither very good nor very bad but clearly appreciated. The crowd pressed closer. A man in the front row leaned with elbows on the stage, a five-dollar bill extended and his nose in the air, hoping to catch the dancer's scent. She arched her back as if doing the limbo and accommodated him, having first collected his money. As the song ended she bowed on a downbeat and announced in a voice that carried to the back of the tent that "dipping time" had arrived. Turner looked intensely uncomfortable, Willy was wide-eyed.

A fresh cigar from the third row was passed to the stage. The dancer waved it through the air, a magic wand, now you see it, now you don't, and placed the cigar between her legs. Men whistled, elbowed each other as the insertion was made. The dancer worked fast, but always with a smile and a rolling of her hips suggesting naughty pleasure. Performances turned over every eight minutes, time for one song and the dipping routine. The cigar was passed back to its owner, who ran it beneath his nose before sticking it in his mouth and striking a match. A bottle was next passed to the stage. The dancer inserted the bottle's neck, in and then out, a corkscrew motion, a twist of the wrist. Again there were whistles, whooping from the rear, down-home Friday-night fun.

"Just one more," the dancer said.

Feeling the urge to participate, his mind racing in search of an object, Willy grabbed Turner's glasses from his face and passed them to the stage. The dancer made a great show of daintily folding the stems, then squatted in plain view and guided the glasses heavenward until they'd disappeared. She stood and tramped across the stage, shaking her ass, stamping her heels, being bad, the glasses lost inside her. This was her finale, after all, the clock winding down. Turner did not react, but then no one was watching Turner. The retrieval was finally made with the dancer on her knees, face contorted as her thumb and forefinger tugged at the heavy plastic frames, burlesque giving birth to an act of mock courage. The glasses were held aloft for all to see before the dancer personally put them back on Turner's face. The lenses were filmy, a mix of natural secretions and K-Y jelly.

Turner was a stone on the drive back to Boston. He didn't move, he didn't speak, and presumably he didn't see, for his glasses lay on the dashboard. Willy drove as if programmed, obeying the speed limit, using his turn signals, trying not to think. He knew he'd blundered, that what had been done might be forgiven but not forgotten. As soon as they got back to the apartment Turner put a pot of water on the stove. When the water was close to boiling he dunked his glasses into the pot.

He'd never been receptive, never plugged-in sexually. There were no dates, no huddled kisses, no walks in the woods. There was no sex because he was in love, or sex because he was lonely and wound tight and sought relief. Centerfolds made no impression. Boys with bandannas, with magnificent asses, passed by unnoticed. There was no furtive peeking at lingerie ads, no rubber products ordered by mail, no triple-X in eight or sixteen millimeter. There was no heat and no static.

Turner lived for his work, pure pursuit, and when he wasn't working he was drinking and watching games on TV. For some unexplained reason he was addicted to televised sporting events. Maybe the beer commercials played a part. Baseball, basketball, football, ice hockey. Team sports. One of the things he liked about living in Texas was that even high school games were on TV. Willy had never shared Turner's fondness for these games. He liked to play but seldom watched. Turner knew this. When they talked on the phone they spoke of sports about as often as they spoke of sex.

If Turner was calling to celebrate and spread word of his good fortune, then surely the joy was work related.

"What's up?" Willy said. "What's the good news?"

"The good news can keep," Turner said. "First I want to know how you're doing."

"Fine, no problems." Which wasn't exactly true. He and Vee hadn't been getting along recently.

"And what about Vee, how's she doing?"

"Fine. We're both all right. Vee's working late at the museum." Working late *again*, he wanted to say.

"I'm glad to hear that. I'm glad to hear there are people other than myself who put in extra hours. Anything else then? Are we all caught up? Nothing more to report?"

Willy didn't bother to answer. This was Turner's way of teasing, his way of showing affection. The more abrupt his manner, the more he tried to dominate conversation, the closer he came to expressing true feeling.

"New topic," Turner said. "What are you drinking?"

"You said there was a celebration. What would be appropriate?"

"Something expensive. I'd suggest Crown Royal, which is what I'm having."

"Doesn't that come in a purple sack?"

"Don't be embarrassed by the sack. I know, you're going to say it's the kind of thing young executives buy their fathers at Christmastime. Well forget all that. The sack's a function of marketing and has nothing to do with the flavor of the whiskey, which happens to be superior in spite of the package it comes wrapped in. I'm drinking Crown Royal—neat, mind you—and chasing it with Chihuahua, a Mexican beer of humble origin. Seems to tone the whiskey down."

"You're saying the Chihuahua makes the whiskey behave." Playing along with Turner.

"There you go. Keeps the Crown honest. We understand each other, we always did."

There were a couple of cans of Rainier ale in the refrigerator. Turner would approve, but the bottle of status quo Imperial on the shelf was not one of your celebration whiskies. Of course

Turner didn't have to know this. He was 1,300 miles away. "I'm all out of liquor," Willy lied. "Let me run down to the corner and I'll call you back in five minutes."

He bought a pack of smokes at the Greek deli, and when he returned he grabbed the ale from the refrigerator and then poured three separate shots of Imperial, using shot glasses with names on them. Lake Tahoe, Denver "The Mile High City," Vancouver Island. The conversation would last as long as his alcohol. Three shots, two cans of ale, no more. He didn't want to get into an argument with Vee later.

"What are we drinking to?" Willy said when he got back on the line.

"Chemistry, Willy. History is being made in my lab."

"I love it." He drank his first shot. "What does chemistry have to do with history?"

"The future of beer may be in my hands. Did you know they brewed beer in ancient Egypt? Beer on the banks of the Nile, isn't that fantastic? Cultures die but beer survives. Think of the Etruscans drinking beer from lead goblets. Think of the Vandals sacking Rome with beer in their bellies."

"How many have you had?"

"What are we talking about? How many *drinks?* I'm celebrating."

Willy drained off his second shot. Turner was way ahead, already in the bag.

"But what are you celebrating? Chemistry, history? I don't get it."

"How many do you think I've had?"

"I think your bottle's getting low."

"The Crown's sinking, is that what you're saying?"

"And I bet you've been hitting pretty hard on those Chihuahuas."

"I've drunk a pack of the little doggies, and why not? The brewery down here doesn't know what to do with me. They can't keep up with the data I've been feeding them. In the last ten days I've discovered seventeen new chemical compounds that occur in the natural course of fermentation. I see Superbeer on the horizon. This is not visionary nonsense, this is real. The brewery's scared shitless. The whole industry could be shaken up."

"Sounds like the brewery ought to be jumping for joy."

"They are, they just want me to go slow. They say they need time to filter the figures. What they don't realize is that I *can't* go slow. I'm pushing the clock."

"What do you mean?"

"Don't ask so many questions. The general manager told me to go home at noon today. He told me to take tomorrow off. The dumb cluck *doubled* my salary. I said no, keep your spare change, I want a piece of the new beer if and when I develop it. Timing could be a problem."

Willy cracked open the second can of ale and drained off his third shot. He was now considering a fourth.

"Turner, this sounds exciting, but I still don't know what part chemistry is playing here."

"Do you really want to hear this?"

"Of course I do."

"You're not just being polite? Normally I can detect that sort of thing in you. Maybe the Crown's getting the better of me."

"Have another Chihuahua."

"Am I drunk? You see I get the feeling you're humoring me. Beer is my *work*, Willy. Chemical compounds, that's the story. In the 1920s, the Germans began to research fermentation. They wanted to *control* beer, to make sure nothing went wrong between the time it was brewed and the time it reached the market. They wanted to enhance the flavor too, but that was secondary. I feel you're still with me."

"I'm right here."

"They thought they'd trace five, maybe six compounds, and guess what? They found ten. I love telling this. By the 1960s, researchers were figuring they'd find as many as a hundred different compounds. They found more. They're still finding them. *I'm* finding them. I'm finding them faster than anybody else. A chromatograph doesn't lie. The count is closing in on seven hundred now. In another couple of years we might crack a thousand, do a Dow Jones."

"What does all this mean?"

"You keep asking. I've got to take a leak. I'm not sure I can still walk. What all this means is that the more compounds we find, the more we can experiment with the flavor of beer. Isolate one group, introduce others. Are you hearing me? Superbeer is not a dream. I've really got to piss, Willy."

"You go ahead. I'm going to pour myself another shot."

Willy wandered off to his kitchen, and when he came back to the phone he waited for Turner's return from the bathroom, but Turner didn't return. Fifteen minutes passed on an open line. Willy nursed his shot, the dregs from his second ale, and waited some more. In the background he could hear rain beating down on the roof of Turner's house. Turner had once said rain fell an average of only three days a year in El Paso. Today was one of those days.

24 · *Medicine*

Willy checked his watch as he heard the key turn in the lock. Almost midnight. He'd been reading on the couch, filling an ashtray, too anxious to go to bed.

"Where have you been?" he said. He couldn't see her. The front door opened onto the hallway, which was around the corner from the living room. He heard her shaking out her umbrella in the bathroom. The day had been dismal, rain since lunchtime, gusting winds.

"I said where have you been? Why didn't you call?"

"I forgot," Vee said from the bathroom. "Give me a minute, I'm soaked."

When she entered the living room she was wearing her half-slip and bra and wrapping a bath towel around her head. Even the slip was wet. She sat on the far end of the couch, opposite Willy.

"Well?"

"Well what?"

She'd been drinking. He could smell alcohol, something hard. Gin, he guessed. "Why didn't you call? Where have you been?"

"I told you I forgot."

"That's ridiculous, Vee."

"Why? I met somebody for a drink after work and I lost track of the time. Don't look like that, Willy. You do the same thing. You're always out. You're always meeting somebody for a drink after work."

"But I call. Don't I always call and let you know when I'll be home? I don't leave you hanging."

"Most of the time you call, sometimes you forget. This was one of my sometimes."

Gin and tonics, he thought. Four, maybe more. And probably no dinner, just bar snacks. "Well what happened? Are you going to tell me or not? How did you get so wet?"

"It's *raining* outside."

Willy sat forward and massaged the back of his neck. He had a cigarette burning in the ashtray. "Couldn't you get a cab?" he said.

"I didn't *need* a cab. Steven had his car, only the car broke down because of all the water. We stalled at a light and couldn't get it started again. I walked the rest of the way home. It was only five blocks."

"Hold on a second. Who is Steven? I don't recall any Steven."

"From the conservation department. He restores objects, cleans paintings. I've told you about him."

"I'm sure I would have remembered, Vee. Who is this guy?"

"He's a *friend*. Sometimes we have lunch together in the museum cafeteria. I needed to talk to him."

"What was so important that you had to stay out until midnight without even calling? Tell me that. And then when you do get home you're all but drunk and soaking wet. You look like a drowned cat."

"*You*," Vee said. She was suddenly on her feet. Willy could see through the wet slip, see the panties beneath. "I was talking about *you*, trying to figure out why you are the way you are. And don't call me a drowned cat. What's that supposed to mean?" She tripped over *supposed*, but otherwise was speaking clearly.

Willy apologized for the remark. Things were getting out of hand.

"Then why did you say it?" Vee persisted. "What exactly were you referring to? That I'm wet? That I was drinking? That I've been slinking around? What? Do you think I was out screwing somebody?"

Jesus, Willy thought. *Drowned cat* was a mistake. Name-calling gets you nowhere. "I haven't said anything about screwing, Vee."

"But were you thinking it? Did you think that's what I'd been doing? You want to check and make sure? You want to smell me?" She managed to step out of the wet slip without losing her balance. "Go on, you want to see if I've been bad? You want to check on your little pussy?"

Maybe she'd been drinking shots. He'd never heard her talk this way before. She was getting madder, working herself into a lather. No, he thought, that's wrong, another mistake. Say *lather* and you'll be in deeper, she'll fling the word back at you. Now she was starting up again.

"Because I've been out late doesn't mean I've been doing anything."

"I know that, Vee."

"Can you say the same? When you call from some bar, tell me you'll be late, how do I know you won't be fucking the first stranger you meet?"

"I don't fuck strangers, Vee."

"No, you buy them a drink first!"

She began to sob, standing alone in the middle of the floor. Her slip was in a pile by her feet. Willy took the towel from her head and dried her hair, then went to the bedroom and got her robe. He helped her put it on, guiding her arms into the sleeves.

"What's this all about?" he said quietly. They were seated side by side on the couch. Vee was shivering. "What have I done to make you so mad?"

"Sometimes when you get home," Vee said, "I hear you trying to climb the stairs. I hear you stumbling, walking into walls."

"I don't come home like that very often."

"Maybe not. But you always have a few, and once you're finally home and I know you're safe, I still worry. It scares me, I think too much."

"What do you think about?"

"About why you do what you do. About the drinking, the carrying on, all the happy hours. It doesn't matter if you call or not. Why aren't you home? Why aren't you with me?"

Willy put his arms around Vee and held her tight. He could think of nothing to say.

"Were you worried when I didn't come home tonight?" she said.

"I couldn't go to bed. I couldn't do anything. I didn't know what had happened to you."

"And what about when I finally got here, when you saw me wet and disheveled and tripping over myself?"

"I didn't like it."

"Now you know," Vee said. Her head was resting on Willy's shoulder, her eyes closed. "Now you've had a taste."

25 · *Dead End*

Turner didn't answer the phone. Never *would* answer the phone again. Turner was dead.

The woman who bought his house and talked to Willy long-distance couldn't tell him how Turner had died.

"Do you know where he might be buried?" Willy asked. He'd called to say hello, see if everything was all right. He hadn't spoken with Turner since that last eerie phone call a couple of months back.

"It's funny," the woman in El Paso was saying, "but your friend was cremated."

Willy pressed the phone receiver to his ear. Precisely what was so funny about being cremated? He waited for an explanation.

"Hello?" the woman said.

"Yes?"

"I was telling you about Mr. Turner being cremated. The only reason I even know all this was because it was mentioned in the *Herald-Post*. He had this funny request."

"I don't know what you mean."

"You know how some people, they want to be buried next to their dog or cat?"

"Yes?"

"Or instead of a casket, they ask to be buried inside their car?"

Silence on Willy's end.

"Well your friend, he was cremated and had his ashes put inside a *beer* bottle, and now the bottle's sitting in a bar somewhere."

"What's the name of the bar?"

"Now how am I supposed to know that?"

"Is it in El Paso?"

"El Paso, maybe Juarez. . . ."

Willy took a cigarette from his shirt pocket and placed it beside the ashtray next to the phone. This was a one-cigarette conversation. One smoke and he was off the line.

"You tell me my friend's ashes are in a beer bottle, that the bottle's in a bar, but you can't tell me the name of the bar or even the *city* where the bar might be located?"

"The newspaper didn't *say*. They said it was a private affair. Nobody knows. But it had to be *somewhere* around here, don't you think? I mean it wouldn't make sense if he was sitting in some bar in *Dallas*, would it?"

Probably not. "So you think he's either in El Paso or Juarez?" Willy said. Talking now as if Turner was a truant husband, a missing person instead of a bar ornament somewhere. He lit his cigarette.

"Well sure, it's pretty much the same city. El Paso and Juarez just spill into each other, even if people don't like to say so. Could be one place as well as the other. Then again, I didn't know your friend, I just bought his house after he died. Maybe he *is* in Dallas. Where did the boy grow up? Was he Texan? Sounds like something a Texas boy might do out of spite."

26 · *Pack It Up*

"Why are you doing this?" Vee said. "I still don't understand."
She looked on as he gathered together a change of clothes,
toiletries, a paperback for the plane. The small canvas suitcase
lay open on the bed. The hour was early, just a few minutes
after seven.

"We went over this last night, Vee. I'm paying my respects,
just as I explained. I'm saying good-bye to a friend, honoring his
memory. How many ways would you like me to say it? What
else is there to understand?"

"Why can't you do that here? Why do you have to travel to
El Paso?" Her arms were crossed, her foot tapping the bedroom
carpet. Her mother used to do that—the crossed arms and nervous foot—whenever she argued with Vee's father. The quar-
rels made an impression on Vee because her parents so seldom
disagreed, though when they did they'd be at it for hours. The
suddenly shrill voices, the faultfinding and blame, would
frighten Vee into action. One time she hid in the crawl space
beneath the back porch until her parents realized she was missing. She made them work to locate her, not uttering a sound, as
quiet as they had been loud. When eventually she was discovered in the beam of a flashlight, her father spoke softly while
her mother coaxed her from the crawl space with open arms.

"Why travel to El Paso? Answer me, Willy."

"Because he *died* in El Paso."

"But where is he? Where are you going to go?"

"I've told you."

"You've told me he's in a bottle of all things, but where, where's the bottle?"

Willy folded a sweater into the suitcase and looked up. "Don't keep on about this, Vee. The bottle's in a bar, you know that."

"*Which* bar? Can't you see where this will lead?"

Willy shook his head.

"You know," Vee said, "I wouldn't be surprised if Turner planned this whole thing. He counted on you to track him down. You'll be having this grand farewell as you get closer and closer to the bottle, one long tribute, a final boozy blowout. Doesn't that sound like him?"

Willy zipped the canvas suitcase. "I'll be back tomorrow afternoon," he said. "Can you pick me up at the airport?"

Now Vee shook her head. The hell I will, she thought. "I was thinking I'd work. I still have a lot to do. . . ."

"You've worked the last three weekends in a row. You must have some time coming to you."

Vee had been cataloguing objects from the museum's antiquities collection. Every day she shifted through dusty bins, through crates packed with bubble wrap, foam, dry excelsior, old newsprint. The history of packing precious artifacts had inadvertently been preserved as carefully as the artifacts themselves. Some objects had been in storage for decades. The museum planned to de-accession a small portion of its holdings in the near future. Vee made notes on what should stay, what might go, and passed them along to her boss, who would seek approval from the museum's board before contacting one of the auction houses. Proceeds from the sale would go towards new purchases. The project had been exciting for Vee, though it involved long hours. Long hours meant fewer hours for anything other than work. Some days Vee worked longer than the project required.

Willy said, "You could always come to El Paso with me. We'd only be gone one day. I wouldn't mind the company."

"What about Turner? The man's dead, and he's still with us. Saying good-bye is one thing, that only seems right. . . ."

"That's what I'm doing."

"That's *not* what you're doing. You're chasing after him, you want a party."

Willy carried his suitcase to the front hall.

"See you tomorrow," he said.

She didn't answer.

27 · *The Search*

Buckled up and sipping airline coffee from a plastic cup, Willy figured the first stop in El Paso would be the brewery where Turner worked. Maybe Turner's boss would know where the beer-bottle urn was hiding. And if he learned nothing there, he thought, he could always drop by the offices of the *Herald-Post*. But then what?

The number of bars and taverns in El Paso would probably fill a page of small print in the phone directory, and Juarez, which was a border tourist town even larger than El Paso, would have more bars than cars, or so Willy imagined. How much ground would he be able to cover in one day? How many bars would he have to visit should he learn nothing at either the brewery or the newspaper? He could piss in the wind and get wet a lot faster.

At the brewery he discovered that Turner worked in isolation in a high-security lab in the building's basement. He had liked it down there. No windows, no secretaries, no one to bother him. Turner's boss, the general manager of the brewery, gave Willy just a few moments of his time. Generous only in his disdain, he said that any man who would deliberately sabotage his memory and good name by having his ashes stored in a beer bottle didn't deserve to be mourned.

Fuck you too, Willy thought.

At the *Herald-Post,* he spoke with an editor who remembered the item that had appeared in the paper. Filler, the editor called it, not even half a column in length. A photocopy was given to Willy, but more the editor couldn't do or say.

Willy read and reread the item and searched for another lead, another angle of penetration. Then an idea gave him pause. The crematorium. How many could there be in El Paso?

Too many, like everywhere else, but only three phone calls later Willy connected and took a cab across town.

River's Edge Funeral Home was set back fifty yards from the Rio Grande. A sign on the front lawn—black with white letters, the kind of sign often posted in front of churches—read "Special Attention Given to Cremations." Willy rang the bell by the front door and walked in.

"You just caught me," the funeral director said. He was a man in his mid-thirties, a few years older than Willy. He wore a short-sleeved yellow knit shirt and a pair of red and white seersucker pants. His face and arms were deeply tanned, his blond hair thinning on top. Willy had expected someone with a dark conservative suit, pallid complexion, manicured nails.

"Another fifteen minutes and I would have been a goner," the director said.

Willy lifted his eyebrows as he shook the director's hand.

"Vista Hills. I was all set to leave when you called."

Vista Hills? Goner? Was this crematory jargon? Willy stared at the director with an empty face.

"You're not from around here, are you?"

"No I'm not."

"Well I won't hold it against you," the director said, chuckling softly. "I play golf over at the Vista Hills club every afternoon. Usually by this hour I'm already gone. You just caught me."

"This will only take a minute."

"No hurry at all. Now about your friend. It's not uncommon for families of the deceased to supply their own urns, but how many people have their ashes placed inside a beer bottle?"

Willy managed a smile. "Must have been a big bottle."

"One liter. I couldn't actually fit all of Mr. Turner inside, but then I don't think he'd have minded, do you?"

"No no, I don't think so. Did the bottle have a label?"

"No label, at least not by the time I got ahold of it. Just a plain brown bottle, nothing fancy about it."

This was the first real information Willy had uncovered, but still it wasn't much to go on. He cleared his throat.

"You wouldn't happen to know how he died, would you?" He recalled the last time he'd spoken with Turner, when there was talk of Superbeer and a shake-up in the industry. Privately he'd been thinking Turner's death might have involved foul play.

"Sure I would," the director said. "Lymphoma."

"Cancer?" Willy said, surprised, the widespread prevalence of the disease, its commonness, somehow making Turner's death more real and terrible.

"That's the one. Attacks the lymphatic system. Very nasty because of the speed with which it spreads. Your Mr. Turner could have given it a try, though."

"Given what a try?"

"Chemotherapy—might have saved his life. Then again it might not have. Who knows? It was worth a shot, an uphill putt, at least from where I'm standing. But no, he wanted to treat himself. He was some kind of chemist, I understand."

Willy nodded. "A very bright guy, one of a kind."

"Not bright enough, don't you think? When I first laid eyes on the man, understand, he looked healthy as you or me."

"When was this?"

"Maybe four months ago."

"But I spoke with him on the phone after that," Willy said. "He never breathed a word. He was very excited about his work."

"Friends and family are often the last to know. He pulled his own strings, didn't he? Got to give him some credit. The man was *sure* of himself. The first time I saw him, he explained the situation and then gave me very specific instructions should his self-treatment fail. I didn't think much about it until the *last* time he dragged himself in here. I want to tell you, a sadder wasted sight you don't often see. Looked like a walking obituary. Tells me to go ahead with our plans. Very polite, not at all upset, almost serene. I think the old boy had been drinking. Gave me a chill up under my scalp. I couldn't play golf that afternoon, and I play golf *every* afternoon. You know what I did instead?"

"What's that?" Willy said, not caring.

"Called my MD and got a physical. Complete rundown. Tests, two days in the hospital, needles in places my wife has never even touched me. Cost a fortune, but I didn't give a damn."

"Can you tell me," Willy said, impatient now, "anything else about the bottle?"

"Like where it is?"

"That's right."

"No I can't. Mr. Turner's instructions were very explicit. Don't ask me why, but that's how it is. Some people request a piece of jewelry or a memento placed inside their urn, but not your friend. The only thing inside that bottle is calcined bone, and the only people who know the location of the bottle are myself, Mr. Turner's lawyer, and the owner of a bar that shall remain forever nameless. And if you're thinking of seeing the lawyer, don't bother. He'll tell you less than I have, and if you get too particular he'll bill you for what he doesn't say."

"You know," Willy began, changing tack, "Turner and I were very close."

The director wagged a finger. "If he wanted you to know where to find him, good buddy, he'd have let you in on the secret, don't you think? I'll tell you this, though. I had a heck of a time getting that bottle through—"

"Through customs? That's it, isn't it? He's in Juarez."

"I didn't say that."

"What are you saying?"

The director shrugged. "Let me put it this way. You'd most assuredly be wasting time if you stayed in El Paso. Now I've got to go, I'm a goner. I've already said too much."

And then a short walk to the bridge, high above the concrete-channeled Rio Grande, and Willy was in Juarez. The feeling as he moved along the street was like strolling into a giant theme park where the motif was not the California Gold Rush or Colonial Williamsburg but delirium of the senses. Boys baked brown by the sun sold cartons of tax free American cigarettes at intersections. Little girls, eyes deep as dark chocolate, squatted on sidewalks and tugged at passing pants legs, begging for pesos. Willy walked along Avenida 16 de Septiembre, past the bustling Mercado, past the foot cops on patrol in their berets and mismatched uniforms. He walked on, past the lush private gardens and the trees with whitewashed trunks and the mazy wrought-iron fences, and felt drunk without even having had a drink.

Which reminded him.

He had to eat and then search for Turner. How long had he been walking? Night had already fallen.

He found a café and took a table on the sidewalk and ordered refried beans, chorizo wrapped in corn tortilla, and a bottle of beer, which was served warm. While he ate he thought again of hopping from bar to bar and was not encouraged. He believed he already knew the outcome of this escapade, this south-of-the-border adventure in pursuit of a man in a bottle. Maybe Vee had been right. Maybe all he was after was a party, a big blowout. And what would he do if he actually found the bottle? Have a drink, of course. Another one.

After paying for his dinner in U.S. currency, Willy walked down the avenue towards the center of the city, imagining how easy it would be to sit at the café for hours, simply watching the traffic and privately drinking warm beer at a slow pace. There was more than one way to say good-bye.

But for all of that the next drink was not beer but tequila, a shot with salt and a wedge of shriveled lime. This was the first bar Willy had entered in Juarez, and after spending ten minutes straining his eyes looking for Turner in the cold dark light, he realized he'd taken far too much time. If he wanted to find the bottle he was going to have to move very fast.

In the next couple of hours he was in and out of twenty-odd bars, drinking beer or tequila in every third or fourth place to keep his ambition fueled. He was still reasonably steady on his feet, still able to speak without a slur and walk without weaving, though once already he'd lit the wrong end of his cigarette and sucked burning filter. That usually happened much later, and he warned himself to ease up on the tequila or his vision might blur, which would be a terrible handicap in dim barlight. He had a clear image of the bottle and believed it would be on display behind the bar top, perhaps near the cash register.

While walking along the sidewalk between the last bar and the next, he heard a car pull softly to the curb. Willy looked over his shoulder and wondered whether he was being followed. A taxi, a late-model Chevrolet Impala with polished chrome and tassels bordering the windshield, stayed close behind him and finally rolled to a stop. Willy stared as an old man opened the front door and stepped out carefully.

"Señor," the man said, grinning as if about to tell a joke, "you are looking for something?"

Willy kept his mouth shut and regarded the cab driver with suspicion.

Laughing easily, the old man walked up to within a foot of where Willy stood. "My name is Hector. You need a guide, no?"

"How do you know I'm looking for something?" Willy said.

"You go into the cantina, but you don't stay. Many cantinas. Por qué? You want chiquita?"

Willy shook his head no and shivered despite the heat. It occurred to him he'd never known anybody named Hector. But then he wondered whether a guide might not be exactly what he needed. Instead of wearing himself down walking from one end of the night to the other, he could be driven in comfort. Not only would he visit more bars this way, he'd also get to the smaller ones off the main avenues. And once drunk, which he knew he would be soon, he wouldn't have to worry about being robbed on the street or picked up by the foot cops. The buddy system, he told himself. Hector would be his buddy, his Mexican compadre.

"How much?" Willy asked.

"You tell me what you want, I tell you how much."

While Willy climbed into the back of the cab, Hector walked around the car and eased himself into the driver's seat.

"I want to go to as many bars as we can," Willy said. "Every bar in Juarez if possible." He looked at his watch, holding it close to his face because of the darkness. Nearing midnight. "We have until tomorrow morning, and then I have to be in El Paso to catch a plane."

Hector looked out the clean windshield of his car, one arm draped over the steering wheel. "Many cantinas will soon close," he said.

"Then we'll go to those that are open. We'll just take our chances and hope Turner shows up."

"Señor?"

"It's a long story. How much?"

Hector swiveled around in his seat and looked at Willy with a face as old as the continent. He was a heavyset man with a splayed nose and great distance between his dark eyes. "Much time, much trouble. I usually not work this late."

"How about twenty-five dollars?"

"I think not," Hector said.

Willy took a booklet of traveler's checks from his back pocket. He had two left—twenties—plus an airline ticket and sixty dollars in cash in his wallet.

"What's your last name, Hector?"

"Ramirez."

Willy made the check out to Hector Ramirez and handed it over the front seat.

Hector turned on the overhead light and looked at the check as if smelling a root pulled from the ground.

"You'll get another twenty, Señor Ramirez, when you deliver me to the border tomorrow."

28 · *Some Sort of Bug*

What Vee did after Willy left for El Paso:

She put a muffin in the oven, then decided she wasn't hungry.

She took a shower and shampooed her hair with conditioner and conditioned her hair with shampoo, reversing the order.

Wake up, she told herself.

She made a fresh pot of coffee and burned her tongue. The scalding was the first thing that morning that didn't bother her.

She dressed for work, then called her boss at the museum and said she wasn't feeling well, which certainly was true.

She changed into jeans and turtleneck and looked out the window, arms crossed, foot tapping.

She called home. Her mother answered. She broke the connection.

Grow up, she told herself.

She thought about being on her own, being alone, what it might be like.

She imagined Willy in bed with another woman. She imagined the woman's hair and body, gave her a perfume. But she wouldn't give the woman a face, that was giving her too much. She started to cry.

Get with it, she told herself. And she finally did. She changed again and dressed for work, arriving at the museum in time for lunch. She bought a cup of coffee at the cafeteria and headed for storage.

The afternoon she spent cataloguing antiquities. Her project was nearing completion. The bulk of what remained, of what hadn't been catalogued, didn't look very promising. *Everything goes*, she told herself. *De-accession the whole lot.* But then she came across a small box bound with blue and gold twine, something she'd previously overlooked. Inside was a second box made of cane, and inside *that* was a small piece of rolled chamois, held together by a bit of knotted string. She pulled the knot, unrolled the packet, and beheld a terracotta cylinder seal not more than an inch in length. Mesopotamia—2400–2000 B.C. She counted four columns of inscription and marveled at the delicately carved figure of a woman in a honeycombed skirt, holding a ewer. Excited, she lifted the cylinder with thumb and forefinger, and that's when the object came apart. Impossible. Two uneven pieces. Just from lifting!

She hurried over to Steven, the conservation man on the second floor. She was distraught. "Can you put it together?" "Sure," he said. But was he *sure?* "Anything can be restored, Vee." "All right," she said, but she was worried. "How are things going?" Steven asked. He was inspecting one half of the broken cylinder with the tip of his pen. "Vee? I said how are things going?" "Willy's in El Paso. Don't ask, Steven, please."

She left work earlier than usual. On the way home she bought a piece of halibut, a potato, and an ear of corn. A plain dinner.

She flipped through the day's mail, changed into jeans and turtleneck, popped her potato in the oven. The oven was still hot. She'd neglected to turn it off in the morning.

Get with it, she told herself.

She made a drink, the kind of drink Willy might make. Whiskey on the rocks, splash of water. "How would you define *splash?*" she'd once asked, teasing. "A splash is a drop," Willy had said. "Any more and you've got a deluge."

She made another. This one she drank slowly.

The phone rang. *Willy?* He sounded like Willy, but then he didn't. "Hi, Matt," she said. Willy's brother. He lived on Long Island, was a CPA with his own business. He'd be in San Francisco next week. "Why don't the three of us have dinner?" he said. Bad timing, Vee explained. Matt wanted to know if anything was the matter. "Willy's in El Paso. Yes, El Paso. Don't ask, Matt. He should be back tomorrow if you want to speak with him. At least I *think* he'll be back tomorrow." A long pause, Vee listening to bees in the line. "I'd hate to see the two of you split up," Matt said. "You go back a long way. I mean you were kids together."

She called the motel in El Paso where Willy had reserved a room. He hadn't checked in yet.

She ate dinner. The corn was tough, but the potato was fine. *What can you do to a potato?* She poked at the halibut.

Is anything the matter? Why yes, now that you mention it. He drinks, he stays out, he thinks pleasure is an occupation.

She washed the dishes. Washing for one was easy. Fast. Five minutes. *What do you do when you're finished?*

She made a shopping list. Dish detergent, paper towels, coffee.

She ironed her linen skirt.

She watched "Hill Street Blues" on television. Captain Furillo annoyed her. Here was this reformed alcoholic who had divorced and then remarried. His work schedule at the precinct was crazy, the pressure and stress incessant. He had a long nose and a beautiful but bitchy wife who called him Pizza Man. God. What was there to like? But what really got Vee was this: every week, every episode, if only for a few minutes, Furillo would emote pain as if he'd absorbed the suffering of all those around him. When he talked he could barely move his little lips. The Captain looked unhappy, profoundly unhappy. *Lighten up, Furillo,* she yelled at the screen. *Lighten up or you'll have a stroke.*

The phone again. Steven. The cylinder seal was back together, looking as old as ever. Vee was grateful, relieved, then suddenly felt selfish, having thrust the seal on Steven in such a rush. "You're not still at the museum, are you?" "Well no," Steven said. He sounded embarrassed. "Actually I'm in a booth around the corner from you, outside of this Greek delicatessen. I thought maybe you'd want to talk. With Willy gone and all." *He wants to sleep with me,* she thought, rolling her eyes. "It's getting kind of late, Steven. I was going to go to bed." "We could do that," he said, hastily making his bid. "But only if you want to."

She rinsed out panty hose in the bathroom sink.

She called the motel in El Paso. Willy hadn't checked in. *The hell with him.*

She washed her face and brushed her teeth. Maybe she'd sleep.

Taking off her clothes, she looked at her profile in the full-length mirror. *Not bad.* At least her body was holding up.

She climbed into bed. With one hand she touched one breast, and with the other hand she touched her other breast. Ron was her left hand, Willy her right. Ron held her breast the way you'd hold a ball. He *gripped* her. Willy was different. Willy didn't so much hold her breast as *cup* it. Very tender. *But then he's had a lot of experience with cups, hasn't he?*

Ron was her left hand, Willy her right. Ron's hand went from breast to belly to being inside her without warming up. . . .

She woke with a start. Had she set the alarm for the morning? The clock on the dresser read 2:32. *I'll get up at 7:45,* she told herself.

She resisted calling El Paso.

She slept.

She was awakened by a police siren and followed the sound as it approached, then receded.

She slept again.

She hit the snooze button three times and got up at 8:30. Late.

She took a shower.

Her panty hose were dry.

She laid out her clothes and then went to the kitchen to put a muffin in the oven. It was still on! The oven had now been burning for twenty-four hours. She turned it off.

Get with it!

Arms crossed, foot tapping.

She called her boss at the museum. Yes, she was feeling poorly again. Some sort of bug.

29 · *Man in a Bottle*

By daybreak Willy had long stopped wondering why he was chasing a dead man down dusty Mexican streets. An hour earlier he'd vomited on the sidewalk, splattering his pants, his shoes. Emptying his stomach had not sobered him for he had continued drinking. On the floor of the backseat was a collection of beer bottles and shot glasses from bars he'd walked out of with drink still in hand. Hector was tired but uncomplaining behind the wheel of his cab, listening to the radio play softly. He had cautioned Willy not to get sick or urinate in the car, that he should use the street when necessary. Abashed, Willy gave Hector his wristwatch as a bonus. Now they were driving north towards the center of the city again.

"How many bars we got left, Hector?"

"I do not know the number exact, but Señor Turner will show up." Hector had concluded, not unreasonably, that they were searching for a man with a beating heart. "If he is not at one cantina, he will be at the next. The sun is up, Willy," Hector now said familiarly, "and the day has eyes the night only dreams of."

Turning left on Avenida Vincente Guerrero, Hector rolled to a stop in front of a bar still lit with green buzzing neon despite near daylight. While Willy went inside, Hector made himself comfortable and dozed in his cab. Another hour or two and he'd bring the American to the border and collect his second traveler's check. As night became day, Willy had lingered longer in each successive bar.

La Esmeralda was a cantina patronized by tourists and young Mexicans with money. Anyone with ten dollars and a leer could go down to the basement and watch an eleven-year-old girl simulate coitus with a tethered burro. At night a band played cover versions of current Top-Forty hits, and strippers danced on a round platform in the middle of the floor. At this early hour, though, the bar was all but empty. In one corner of the barroom was a booth with a bilingual sign and a red and orange curtain over the entrance, and behind the curtain was a tattoo parlor run by a transplanted Canadian who called himself a "needle artist."

Willy sat slumped on a bar stool and ordered a shot of tequila, waving away the saltshaker and lime the bartender brought him. He drained the tequila and absently put the shot glass in his shirt pocket, then ordered a beer.

"Make that two, Luis," said a voice behind Willy. It was the needle artist, slim, his skin gray in the early light, come from his booth for a fast beer before going home to bed. He'd be back late in the evening, when the bar was crowded and customers had to take numbers to get tattooed.

The needle artist sat at a stool two down from Willy and said, "I bet you've been having one wild time."

"Looking for Turner," Willy said, though he hadn't looked for Turner since entering the bar. He'd forgotten.

"Been looking long?"

"Only all fucking night. He's in a bottle, if you can believe that shit." Alcohol had washed the polish from Willy's tongue. He was beyond sloppy.

"In a bottle," the needle artist repeated evenly. His trade was with drunks, mostly young men, though occasionally he'd get some wacked-out girl who wanted a butterfly on the cheek of her ass. Very little surprised the needle artist. Taking a pen from his shirt pocket, he quickly sketched a long-necked wine bottle on a cocktail napkin, then slid over one stool. "Is your buddy in a bottle like this?"

Willy shook his head. "Beer bottle."

The needle artist sketched another bottle, complete with a Dos Equis label.

"No label."

And then a third sketch on a third napkin, drawn faster than the previous two.

"That's the bottle, that's what I'm looking for, only there's a guy inside."

The needle artist put a little man inside the bottle. "Your friend is in a bottle like this?"

Willy closed his eyes and began to weave erratically on his stool. Soon he pitched forward, grazing his cheekbone against the sharp edge of the bar top.

"Your friend," the needle artist said again, propping Willy back up, "is in a bottle like this one?" Pointing to the sketch with his pen, all business. He ignored the blood that was beginning to ooze from Willy's cheek and continued talking. "Would you like a bottle like the one I've just drawn for you? One to take back home? To keep as a souvenir?" Talking now with a little oil in the voice, trying to close the deal smoothly.

Willy tried to think. "You're the tattoo guy, right? I saw you walk out of that booth."

"I'm a needle artist."

"Whatever." He took a couple of bills from his pocket, a ten and a five, and then a handful of Mexican and U.S. coins, and put them on top of the bar. The airline ticket, last traveler's check, and a wad of small bills were still in his wallet.

"You must have more money than that," the needle artist said.

"This is it. You going to help me or what?"

Some customers were so blind and stinking sodden they just handed their wallets over to the needle artist, Master Charge and all. He was disappointed in Willy, but nevertheless led him to the booth behind the red and orange curtain.

Willy sat in an old padded leather chair, what was once a barber's chair, and sucked at the beer in his hand. Maybe he hadn't found Turner, but he'd gotten as close as he was going to get. The blood on his cheek had by now coagulated.

"If you just sign this slip of paper," the needle artist said, "which permits me to practice my trade, I'll get this disaster over with. You want this bottle, right?" He held the sketch very close to Willy's face.

Willy nodded, smiled with closed eyes. Abuse from the needle artist could not reach him.

"And where do you want this tragedy? The biceps?"

Willy nodded again. The search was over. While he took off his shirt, fingers fumbling with the buttons, the needle artist bent over his messy tray of dyes and needles and rubbing alcohol, still in disarray from a busy night.

"How about using a couple of colors," Willy suggested, his speech an advanced slur. "Make the fucker two-tone."

The needle artist stared Willy in the face as if he'd been asked to do a tattoo replica of the Eiffel Tower.

"Not for fifteen bucks and change I won't," he said indignantly. "Anyway, you smell like a sick dog."

30 · *Home*

She had prepared herself, but even so. He could have been dead as he lay stretched across three seats in the arrivals area of the airport. No one sat near him, though the room was busy. His shirt was free from his pants, his hair matted and wild, so crazy he might have been fashionable. Even from this distance, thirty feet, twenty feet, still making her approach, she could see the shirt was buttoned wrong.

He wore the same clothes he'd worn yesterday morning. Where was the canvas suitcase? Getting closer, she could see scattered stains down the front of his pants, see the sock that had worked its way into the heel of his shoe. There was something wrong with his cheek. An abrasion, a raw patch. Had he fallen? Had he been in a fight?

Closer still, bending over, she smelled stale alcohol, but there was more, another odor prevailing, a powerful sourness. She touched his shoulder, a gentle prod with the tips of her fingers.

His eyes opened immediately, the lids blinking back light, though his body remained inert. Only his eyes seemed alive.

"I didn't think you'd come," he said, his voice trailing off. "But I was hoping. . . .

She leaned further into him, deep into the sourness, and kissed his cheek, kissed the raw patch of skin.

"Let's go home," she said.

31 · *Specimens*

And things got better.

He was bathed and put to bed and slept through the day. When he woke he was fed and the dressing on his cheek changed. When he dared smile, when he dared look her in the eye, she held his gaze without reproach. Turner and El Paso and the lurid tattoo were not mentioned. The bad feeling and mistrust that had passed between them were not mentioned. In fact little was said, though he understood from her kindness and care that there now existed a tacit belief in the future. He belonged to her, they belonged to each other, and together they might be happy.

Within days a routine was established. Vee began working normal hours at the museum, and in the evenings, Willy found his pleasure back at home, with her. They ate in, they read in bed, they even danced to the radio. Almost any book or song would do. They were easy to please and all seemed well, better perhaps than Willy had a right to expect, until one alarming Sunday morning nearly two months later.

Orange pekoe steeping in hot water.

This is what Willy's urine reminded him of. Tea. Steaming in the porcelain toilet bowl like a giant cup of Lipton's finest.

"Vee," he called from the bathroom.

She was curled up in the bedroom, a blanket pulled over her shoulders. Sunday was the one day she slept in, her day to be lazy, rarely rising before ten or even eleven. Sunday mornings Willy slipped out of bed about eight and went down to the corner for the paper.

He called her again and kept his eyes on the bowl, amazed and fearful of the discovery he'd made and needing to share the newness of it. A minute later he heard the rubber slap of Vee's flip-flops on the wooden floor as she made her way to the bathroom. Her long flannel nightgown, kept at the foot of the bed while she slept, was pinned to her chest and the front of her body with her hands. She looked chilly. One side of her face was creased from having been pressed into the mattress.

"What is it?" she said. She stared at Willy, at his eyes.

"Look," he said, taking her by the arm, pulling on her, leading her to the toilet. "Look at that."

Vee was not entirely awake as she bent over and peered into the murk. "Rusty water," she said. "Is it a bad pipe?" Whenever they went away for more than two days at a time, the tap in the kitchen sink ran rust-colored water for a full five minutes after they opened the spigot. "We can call the super later," she said. "What time is it, anyway?"

"I don't know what time it is, I just got up. Will you look at that, please." Still holding Vee's arm. "That's *me.* I pissed that mess into the bowl not two minutes ago."

Vee made coffee while Willy sat in the living room and smoked, but after two short drags he stubbed his cigarette into the tray. Why were cigarettes suddenly tasting like wet ash? And why was he feeling so tired, as if he'd just run laps around the block? He didn't want to move. For the last few days he'd noticed a creeping ache in his elbows and knees.

Vee brought coffee from the kitchen, sipping at her own cup as she sat down next to Willy. A moment passed before she said, "You look sort of yellow, Willy."

He didn't answer.

"I mean it. Go to the bedroom mirror and see."

"I think I'll just sit for a while," he said. "Maybe you could get me that hand mirror of yours."

Vee rooted through her leather handbag in the hall and came back carrying the compact case with the circular mirror.

"You're right," he said. "I look like I was born on the other side of the world." He studied his face in the small mirror and pulled down on the pouch beneath one of his eyes. "And my eyes. Have you noticed? The *whites* are yellow. Not by the pupils, but around the edges."

Vee patted Willy's knee, rubbed his shoulder, sipped her coffee, one nervous gesture succeeding the next.

"I'd like to know what's going on," he said quietly. "I wake up and take a leak and all of a sudden my body's on red alert. How come? What have I done this time?"

Vee walked across the room to the phone. "I'm calling the doctor," she said.

Willy shook his head slowly. "I don't *have* a doctor."

Typical Willy. He ordered special vitamins from a pharmaceutical house in Seattle and did half an hour of calisthenics every morning, but he didn't have a regular doctor.

"I'm calling *my* doctor," Vee said. "She gave me her home number in case of emergency."

"I don't think we're in an emergency situation here, Vee." Hedging now. Ever since his father had died he'd been suspicious of doctors. After the first heart attack the cardiologist had told him his father was going to be all right. Myocardial infarction was a term new to Willy. Hospital corridors made him dizzy. He appreciated the doctor's soothing tone and slept well that night. But twelve hours later his father was gone and his mother stuttered whenever she opened her mouth.

"Willy," Vee said, "you just told me you wanted to know what was going on. How can you be sure this isn't serious? Look what happened to Turner."

She punched out the number on the Touch-Tone phone. The doctor was out, but Vee left a message on a machine. Later that afternoon her call was returned and an appointment was scheduled for eight-thirty the following morning.

"She wants to see both of us," Vee told Willy.

He was still in the same chair he'd been sitting in since morning, now with a blanket over his hunched shoulders. The Sunday paper was scattered in sections by his feet. Vee had gone down to the corner after making breakfast. Willy hadn't been able to eat. Loss of appetite, nausea, more symptoms of a nameless disorder. To name is to know, to have something to blame.

"Why both of us?" Willy said.

"She wants blood tests. We're supposed to bring urine specimens, too."

"But I'm the one who's sick."

"Don't worry. I'll be a little late for work, that's all."

While Willy sat and stared out the window, Vee rummaged beneath the kitchen counter. He could hear her shifting pots and pans, clinking glasses, lifting silverware by the handful. The colander fell from one of the shelves and wobbled on its rim along the floor. Its hard metallic sound gave Willy a chill that danced down his spine.

"Do we have any empty jars, Willy?"

"There's a couple of old jam jars I use for making Irish coffee," he said. "For whipping the cream."

"Where are they?"

"On the middle shelf." Willy's fondness for Irish coffee on wet and windy weekend afternoons took his mind away from his condition. "Actually you *shake* the cream," he said. "You don't want to whip it."

"I can't find them."

"They're on the middle shelf, near the cheese grater. But I don't want you to use those jars for our urine specimens, Vee. We've got other jars around somewhere." He went back to Irish coffee, speaking softly but with an enthusiasm that made his eyes shine. "Some people use a blender and just beat the shit out of the cream until it's nothing but air. What they don't realize is that your cream needs a little weight. Your cream should really *sit* on top of the coffee, not hover. Of course using a blender is better than shooting cream from an aerosol can. That's just about the worst. If we're ever in a bar, Vee—"

She poked her head above the counter. "We don't go to bars anymore, remember? If you want to drink you can do it at home, with me."

"I know. I'm just saying *if*, a rhetorical *if*. *If* we're ever in a bar and we happen to see the bartender making Irish coffee with a can of Redi-Whip, we've got to leave as fast as we can. We've got to get out and never go back to that place again. I mean never. You can't be too principled about this sort of thing. Hey Vee?"

She disappeared, though he heard running water from the bathroom.

"Vee? You're not pissing into one of my Irish coffee jars, are you? We'll find something else."

Vee slunk into the living room with her hands behind her back and mischief all over her face. She could have been five years old.

"I had to go," she said. She held up one of the jam jars.

"Yours is yellow," Willy said.

The next morning Vee steered Willy out the door and folded him into the backseat of the car. He hardly had the energy to slip into clothes and a pair of loafers. He hadn't brushed his teeth or combed his hair. He hadn't smoked a cigarette or taken his vitamins. Calisthenics were out of the question.

In the doctor's office Vee helped him fill out medical and insurance forms. A nurse then brought them to the examination room behind the reception area and drew blood from their arms. Afterwards she asked for their urine samples. Willy instructed her to return the jam jars when she was through with them.

"He's only kidding," Vee said.

Willy was in no mood to kid. He'd been irascible since yesterday morning.

While Vee went back to the reception area with the nurse, Willy climbed onto a green padded table in the brightly lit examination room. His hands and armpits were clammy.

"I'm Doctor Carey," an attractive woman of about forty said, entering the room from a door adjoining her private office. She was tall, six one or two, and wore a new pair of running shoes and a starched lab coat with a stethoscope protruding from the pocket. She walked over to the padded table and briskly shook Willy's hand. Like many doctors, she appeared to be in a great hurry. Her face was scrubbed and free of makeup, though around her neck she wore a slender gold chain, and around her wrist a black-plated digital watch. She looked healthy and sporty and sure of herself.

Willy felt like a bag of bones packed with sickness.

"Well?" the doctor said. "What seems to be the problem?" She held a pen and aluminum clipboard in her hands.

Willy listed his symptoms in a low brooding voice while the doctor made notations. "Go on," she kept saying, "go on," writing quickly as he detailed his disorder. Finally she looked up.

"Are you a drug user?" There was no blame in her voice, no real curiosity. The question was as neutral as another. *Are you a swimmer? Do you remember what you ate for dinner last night?*

Willy had been slouching as he sat on the edge of the table, but now he straightened his back.

"Drugs," she said again. "Have you ever taken drugs intravenously? Yes or no."

"No," he said.

The doctor snagged a loose strand of hair from her forehead and tucked it back behind her ear. "Fine. Why don't we take our shirt off. I want to listen to your heart."

Willy felt the fatigue in his muscles, the ache in his joints, as he unbuttoned his shirt.

The doctor crooked her neck, trouble crossing her face. "And what might this be?" She pointed with her stethoscope.

Later Willy would recall that at that precise moment, just as the doctor was asking the question, even before she had finished speaking, the source of his illness had been revealed to him. He saw the unwashed hands and the bent shape of the needle artist as he had stooped over his messy tray of dyes and needles. He remembered sunrise in dusty Juarez, an empty bar, a room behind a bright curtain. He remembered Hector, who not only got him to the border but somehow put him on the plane in El Paso. Willy had been drunk and nearly delirious.

"I've got hepatitis," he said evenly. He focused on the narrow lapels of the doctor's lab coat.

"It sure looks that way, sailor." She smiled for the first time. "You've got all the symptoms of hepatitis B. We'll know for sure this afternoon when I get the results of your blood and urine samples back from the lab." And then she used her stethoscope once again as a pointer. "When did you have the artwork done?"

"Wait a second," Willy said. "Did you say *sailor*? Was that meant to be funny? I'm sick and you're cracking jokes?"

"It's supposed to put you at ease. Some patients are reassured when they hear a doctor joking at a critical moment. Forget I said it. I need to know when."

"The tattoo?"

"What do you think?"

"Seven or eight weeks ago," Willy said, disgusted with himself, the doctor, the world. "You don't want to hear about it." He picked up his shirt from the table and put it back on with effort.

"But I *do* want to hear about it. I want to know everything you can tell me. That *thing* on your arm is why you're here." Her pen was ready. "Start talking."

"He really ought to be in the hospital," Dr. Carey was saying. "But if you can promise he'll stay in bed and do nothing until I say so—and I mean nothing, Vee, not even a walk around the block to get a quart of milk—then I think it will be all right to take him home. For the next week or so I'm going to have a nurse stop by your apartment every morning and take a blood sample and check how Willy's doing. The nurse will be expensive, but she'll be cheaper than the hospital."

"Why can't I take Willy's blood myself?"

"Maybe you can, though we won't know for at least a week. You're asymptomatic, but that doesn't mean you're immune. And even if you were immune, you may still be a carrier. Have you and Willy had sex recently?"

Vee nodded. Three days ago. Willy had been sluggish. Normally he was more athletic in bed. She remembered that afterwards he'd fallen asleep while he was still inside of her.

"Well I'm afraid the fun and games are going to have to stop for a while," the doctor said.

"How long is a while?"

"A while is a while. I'll let you know."

"This is going to be hard on Willy." Vee was thinking of herself as well. Her appetites may not have been as constant as his, but there were times when she could be very insistent.

"He can barely dress himself without wanting to stop and rest. What kind of lover do you think he'll be in bed?"

Woman to woman talk here. Vee smiled to be polite.

"Another thing," the doctor said, "and this is very important. He can't drink any alcohol. Absolutely none. I know he's depressed and cranky about all of this, but his liver's severely inflamed. One of the complications from hepatitis can be cirrhosis."

"Does Willy know?"

"I just told him."

Vee nodded, but she was already thinking of ways to make life easier for him during his convalescence. "How about a glass of wine with dinner?" she suggested.

The doctor frowned and looked down at her new running shoes. "*After* Willy's better he can have a glass of wine with dinner. Fair enough? And if he wants a beer with a sandwich every now and then, fine, who am I to refuse a reasonable man?" She crooked her neck. "Understood?"

Vee understood only too well. When Dr. Carey finally escorted her to the reception area, they found Willy slumped in a chair and fast asleep, his mouth hanging open.

"He's all yours," the doctor said.

32 · *Her Lips*

Vee never did catch Willy's hepatitis, nor did she become a carrier of the disease, though carrier was a good word to describe her function. Willy had been confined to bed for four long weeks, then sat around the apartment another three, doing nothing more strenuous than retrieve the day's mail from the lobby of the building and talk with his office and Augie Thom down at Pier 18. He was following doctor's orders, doing exactly as the doctor prescribed, which hardly lightened Vee's load.

Every morning she drew a sample of Willy's blood and dropped it off at the lab for analysis on her way to the museum. She shopped for food on her way home at night, cooked dinner, washed dishes. On Saturdays she hauled a sack of dirty clothes to the laundromat and then bought fresh fruit and vegetables from the greengrocer. She kept the apartment clean, made the bed, borrowed books for Willy from the public library. She bought him newspapers and magazines and mints. Willy had taken to sucking mints while he read. Maybe the habit shouldn't have irritated Vee, but it did. A lot of things irritated her. His elaborate shopping lists. His instructions for cooking this meal or that. And as he regained his health he grew ever more cheerful. Under such circumstances good cheer was not easily reciprocated.

But then something happened. Early one morning word arrived, deliverance by telephone, bringing news they'd both been waiting for. Dr. Carey explained Willy's blood was nearly clean and his liver no longer inflamed.

They both got on the line, Willy in the living room, Vee on the extension in the bedroom.

"Let's give it a few more days," Dr. Carey said, her manner busy and professional, somehow washed of emotion. Vee imagined her brushing a strand of hair from her forehead, maybe flicking her wrist to glance at her digital watch. "And I want you to start taking long walks in the afternoon," she told Willy. "You need to build up your strength. Barring complications, I think you can return to work next week."

No sooner were they off the phone than Willy suggested a celebration.

"How about a restaurant, Vee? Do you want to eat out Friday night?"

She sat on the edge of the sofa while Willy reclined, his feet on the cushions and his fingers laced together behind his head. To Vee he looked rested and fit, younger than his years. She'd been in the kitchen when the doctor phoned, tending to dinner, wondering how much more drudgery she could withstand. But the doctor's call, coming at just the right moment, had the effect of a balm. Dinner away from the apartment, a meal she wouldn't have to cook, sounded like Christmas.

"I'd love to," she said, the tightness already diminishing at the back of her neck, leaving her shoulders. She got down on all fours and pulled an old restaurant guide from the bottom shelf of the bookcase. "Where should we go?"

"Your choice," Willy said. "Anywhere at all. I'm not particular as long as the restaurant has a liquor license."

"Willy."

"What? Doctor Carey said I could have a drink with dinner as soon as I was better. You told me that yourself."

"One drink. I'm going to be strict about this."

"I expect nothing less. Are we pals or not?"

"We're pals, you know we are, but that has nothing to do with having a drink."

"We're pals forever, Vee. And we trust each other, don't we?"

She nodded.

"Then listen. Why wait until Friday night to celebrate?"

"I'm not sure I like the sound of this, Willy. I know Doctor Carey wouldn't."

"Screw Doctor Carey. I'm talking about us. Anyway, you trust me, you just said so. There's a bottle of wine in the cupboard, Vee. Why don't you uncork it."

"Willy."

"Not for me, for you."

"And what are you going to do?"

He tapped the side of his nose.

"I don't understand," she said.

"All I'm asking is that you drink a glass of wine. A simple request, no?"

She was on her feet again, beginning to smile, the restaurant guide still in hand. "And then what? What are you up to?"

"And then," Willy said, "we go to bed, we roll around, and you let me smell the wine on your lips. Do I hear a yes?"

"Yes," Vee said.